To my own Doan Riley.

Cinderella Steals Home
Copyright 2013 Carly Syms
All rights reserved.

http://carlysyms.com
Twitter: @carly_syms

Cover Art: Katie Murray, Mumbo Marketing

I flick the blinker on my beat-up, two-door forest green Honda and pull into the left turn lane. I stare out the windshield at the landscape in front of me and can't stop a long sigh from escaping my lips.

"Toto," I mutter to the empty car. "We're definitely not in Pennsylvania anymore."

A tall, wide mountain range rises in the distance and the lowering sun casts a red glow across the rugged terrain. The sun darkens the outline of the cacti that litter the mountainside. Palm trees line the streets in front of me, and even at almost five in the afternoon, I can't find a cloud in the bright blue sky.

It's been almost a decade since I've seen the desert and I'm not all that happy to be back again, but here I am. It's not like I had any real choice in the matter -- it was either moving back to Arizona or crashing at my grandma's house in Toronto, and I'm not about to cross any international borders anytime soon.

So, the southwest won out in the end and that's why I currently sit in my dented old car in the middle of Scottsdale right alongside BMWs and Jaguars and Range Rovers, but I don't care if I look out of place. I'm not trying to fit in here.

The light changes from red to green and I turn left, my GPS alerting me that I'm only five miles from Dad's house in the Phoenix suburbs. I accelerate -- as well as my trusty old car will let me, anyway -- up the street when a red Mustang with its top down and a shiny black pick-up truck scream through the red light and career wildly into traffic, the squeal of tires ringing in my ears.

I slam my foot on the brakes to avoid plowing into the back of the SUV in front of me, a choice string of curses pouring out of my mouth. The red Mustang almost crashes into a minivan a few cars ahead of me but it zooms around it at the last second, rides the tail of the truck and cuts back into the left lane before speeding up and taking off again.

My jaw drops and without even thinking about it, I immediately push down on my gas pedal to catch up to these idiots to let them know exactly what I think of them. It's what I would have done in Pennsylvania, anyway, and I see no reason not to do the same thing now. I can hardly believe what I'm watching.

The two cars continue to weave in and out of traffic until they come to a red light. The Mustang blows through it again, almost causing another accident, but the driver of the pick-up slams on the brakes so hard that the truck screeches to a halt in a cloud of smoke, burning rubber and shame.

Determined, I weave around several cars, pulling up along the truck and roll my window down.

"Hey!" I yell at the pick-up. The dark tinted windows make it impossible to tell who's driving, or if they even notice me shouting. I honk my horn twice and finally the passenger side window lowers.

"What the heck was that?" I scream without seeing who's behind the wheel.

The driver leans over into the passenger seat and my mouth runs dry, rage momentarily subsiding as my brain scrambles to make sense of what's happening.

A gorgeous -- and trust me, I don't use the term lightly -- guy with dark blonde hair and tan skin and beautiful warm golden eyes looks back at me.

He hits me with a perfect white smile and I can't take my eyes off the ripple of his biceps beneath the gray Coyotes T-shirt that clings to his arms.

But then I remember him blowing through the red light and it's easy to get mad all over again.

"Are you insane?" I demand.

"Something the matter, sweetcheeks?" he asks, flashing me the smile I know he's used on countless girls before. He looks like the type who knows he can charm anyone, anywhere.

And I'm sorry to admit it almost works again.

"Do you not know what you just did?" I point back toward the traffic light behind us.

He glances over his shoulder. "Oh, that?" He shrugs. "Eddie and I were just racing, that's all. No harm, no foul."

My eyes bug out of my head. "No harm, no what?" I cry. "You could have killed someone."

"I could have been killed, too," he replies so simply that it sends chills running down my arms. He pats his chest. "But, oh, look, no one's dead and here I am, still in the flesh. Aren't you lucky?"

"Yeah, well, just because you might have a death wish doesn't mean everyone else who shares the road with you does, too," I snap. "Don't be such an asshole."

Something flickers across his face then -- remorse, maybe, I'm not sure -- but it's quickly replaced with another cocky smile that I find repulsive.

Or at least I tell myself I find it repulsive.

"Aww, come on, princess, you don't even know me," he says with a wink. "You might be right about the asshole thing but at least grab a beer with me before you decide for sure."

I laugh. "Now *I'd* rather die," I say before jabbing my finger against the window button. I face forward and wait for the light to turn green without looking back at him even though I know he's still watching me through the window.

I have no time for idiots like this. I know too many of them from back in Pennsylvania.

Leaving them behind might be the only good thing about this whole move. Too bad it looks like they followed me out here.

The light changes and his black pick-up truck speeds past my car. I crawl along at a safe pace until I lose him and the GPS directs me into a neighborhood off the main road.

I drive through the development of sprawling, expansive houses and realize my car is chugging just a little too hard as it tries to get up this mountain.

Finally, the GPS dings and I ease to a rest along the curb in front of, well, in front of a mansion.

My dad's house is undeniably beautiful with its Spanish-style architecture and light red stucco walls.

I let out another sigh. I really don't want to do this.

But it isn't like I have a choice anymore.

I made my decision.
This is it.
My new home sweet home.

CHAPTER ONE

I pull the key out of the engine and take a deep, steadying breath. The longer I can draw this out, the better. I'm just about to take the GPS off the dashboard and put it away when I see him.

He's taller in real life than he is in my memories.

His blonde hair looks darker now, his clothes definitely more upscale. The man I once knew didn't wear pressed khakis and polo shirts and golf visors, but I guess that's who he is now.

But he's still my father.

"Holly!" Dad walks over to my car and has the driver's side door open before I even know what's happening.

In a daze, I unbuckle my seatbelt and turn to get out of the car. He takes a step back to let me out and give me my space, which I appreciate.

But the second my feet hit the ground, he's wrapping me up in a big bear hug -- the kind I used to love when I was six.

So much for personal space and easing back into things.

"Hi...Dad."

He lets go and looks at me. "How the heck are you? It's so good to see you, kiddo."

"I'm fine."

"Let's go inside." He puts his arm around my shoulders and takes a step forward. I don't move.

"I should get my bags first."

"Don't worry about that," he says. "I'll have your brother do it. Come on, I want to show you the house."

I follow him up the driveway, past the gates that lead to an outdoor front courtyard like the one we used to have years ago and through the entryway.

"Oh," I say once I step inside. "This is really nice."

And it is. A far cry from the place Mom and I had moved to in Pennsylvania. That house isn't bad but we've been living a life of poverty compared to what Dad's got going on here in the desert.

We walk into a marble foyer with a winding iron staircase that leads to a loft overlooking the entry and the backyard. Curved archways lead to a maze of hallways and I can already see an infinity pool overlooking the edge of the mountain that the house is built into through the floor-to-ceiling windows in the living room.

"It's your home now, Holly."

"Maybe just my house," I say quickly.

He looks over at me. "Whatever you want, of course," he says, but it's hard to miss the change in his voice.

Dad's new wife appears in the loft and walks over to the landing.

"Holly!" The blonde woman immaculately coifed and dressed in head-to-toe white linen smiles brightly at me before she walks down the steps, the heels of her stilettos pinging off the iron staircase. "It's wonderful to see you!"

"Hi Tanya," I say politely. I haven't seen her since she married my dad in Hawaii five years earlier.

"How are you *doing*, darling?" she asks, placing her hands on my shoulders and air kissing my cheeks.

In my almost ten years of living in Pennsylvania, I'm pretty sure I've never seen an air kiss. I struggle not to roll my eyes -- I know it'll hurt Dad's feelings if he sees and while I don't really want to be here, I don't want to be a total brat to him, either. He's giving me a place to live and saving me from a move to Canada, after all.

"Good, Tanya. And I guess I should say congratulations."

"Wonderful," she says, clapping her hands together before moving them to her still-tiny belly. "And thank you, darling." She looks over at Dad and beams. "We couldn't be more thrilled about the baby. I'll go see about some lemonade in the kitchen. You must be thirsty after that long drive."

"Have you seen Justin?" Dad asks before she leaves the room.

"He's out back."

Dad turns and walks through one of the archways, motioning for me to follow him.

We head down a long, narrow hallway and suddenly we're out on the back patio. I'd been right about the infinity pool but I'm even more blown away by the view in front of me.

Dad's house is built into the side of a mountain and we're about halfway up, which gives us a pretty incredible way to see the Valley. I can even make out the Phoenix skyline from our deck.

I hear the splash before I see it coming but suddenly, my jeans and red T-shirt are completely soaked.

"What the...?"

"Justin!" Dad barks, and I snap my head up.

And there he is, shaking his head to get the water droplets out of his eyes. My big brother Justin.

I haven't seen him since the wedding, either.

"Sorry, Dad," Justin says, then he looks over at me and his eyes grow wide.

Before he can say anything, a shrill female voice yells, "Look out below!" A few seconds later, another giant splash rises up from the pool water and soaks the deck.

A tanned dark-haired girl dressed in a white bikini pops up from the water and brushes her hair back with a giggle.

"Did you see me, Justin? How'd you rate my splash? Perfect ten like always, right?"

It takes her a second to realize she has an audience.

"Oh!" she says, catching sight of me and my father. "Hi, Mr. Shaw."

Dad's shoulders twitch like he's trying not to sigh too loudly. "Hello, Katie," he says in a less-than-pleasant tone. "Justin, your sister's home."

Justin hasn't taken his eyes off me since he first noticed me standing here. He looks like he isn't really sure how to react to seeing me.

I have to say, I know the feeling.

But he gets over it pretty quickly.

"Holly! It's really you!" He swims over to the edge of the pool nearest me and hoists himself out of the water and runs over, flinging his arms around me.

"Ugh, Justin, you're all wet."

He shrugs and laughs. "So are you."

I sigh and roll my eyes, but it's hard not to smile. He's still the same goofy big brother I remember all those years ago even if I haven't lived with him in almost a decade.

"How ya doin', kid?" he asks.

"I'm good," I say, and it's mostly true. I'm not bad, anyway. "How are *you*?"

"Meh," he replies. "Could be worse. How's Mom?"

This time, I can't stop the sigh from slipping out between my lips. "She's happy."

He nods once. "Good," he says, then takes a step back and makes a grand sweeping gesture at the yard and pool. "What's mine is yours. Make yourself at home."

"Don't forget our dinner plans tonight, Justin," Dad says sharply.

"Yeah, yeah, Dad, I got it. You only told me twelve times today."

"I wouldn't remind you if I didn't think I had to."

I look back and forth between them. There's an obvious tension here, one that I know nothing about, but I've got a feeling I'm about to become all too familiar with it.

"Holly," Dad says, turning to me with a smile. "We thought we would have dinner together tonight. You me, Tanya and Justin, that is. Whadda ya say?"

Truthfully, I haven't given much thought to what I'd do for meals out in Arizona at all, so if Dad's offering, I'm not really in a position to say no. Even if I'd probably rather avoid the one-big-happy-family thing for as long as I can.

"Sure, that'll be great."

Dad nods, satisfied. "Justin, get your sister's things out of her car and put them in her room."

"I have company." Justin nods to Katie, who's taken to sunning herself on the pool's tanning ledge. She doesn't look particularly interested in our family reunion.

"Now," Dad says, tossing a dry towel at him.

Justin sighs and drapes it across his shoulders. "Car keys?" he asks me.

I dig them out of my back pocket and toss them to him. He snags them out of the air with ease.

"Be right back," he says to Katie, who just waves her arm in response without looking up.

Lovely.

I'm pretty sure she has an easier time making herself at home in my dad's house than I ever will.

"I'm going to help your brother," Dad says to me. "Why don't you head upstairs and pick any of the bedrooms you like? They're all free except for Justin's, and I don't think you'll have a problem figuring out which that is."

I nod. "Okay. Thanks."

He smiles at me, obviously thrilled with how this afternoon has unfolded so far, before following my brother around to the front yard.

I stand here for a minute, trying to collect myself with deep breaths, when Katie pushes herself up onto her elbows and lifts her sunglasses to look at me.

"Where'd you come from anyway?" she asks.

"Pennsylvania."

"Oh." She doesn't look impressed. "Why?"

"My mom moved to Europe with her new husband," I reply, not blinking an eye. "I didn't have a choice."

She nods sympathetically. "My dad takes his girlfriends to Italy all the time," she says, cracking her gum. "I know how you feel."

I look at her, surprised to find an ally in such an unlikely place. "Sucks, right?"

She shrugs. "He leaves me the Benz when he goes so it isn't that bad."

Okay, maybe not.

"I'll see you later," I tell her and wander inside.

I want to explore the house but I know Tanya's around somewhere and my dad and Justin will be back inside with my suitcases in a few minutes and I don't want them to think I'm a snoop.

Best just to head upstairs and pick out a bedroom like he told me.

I tiptoe up the iron stairs, not wanting to attract any extra attention, and open the first door I find. Linen closet. The second is a bathroom.

Behind door number three is a bedroom with pink walls, pink bedding and pink curtains. Nope.

I open what I'm pretty sure is Justin's bedroom next. It looks lived in: drum set, acoustic guitar, baseball posters on the walls, T-shirts on the floor.

Interesting that my brother is apparently a musician.

I don't remember that about him.

When I open the next door, I know instantly that I've found my bedroom. I don't need to see the others. The walls are painted beige to match the simple white, fluffy-looking comforter with tan accent pillows. The queen-sized bed takes up most of the room, but that isn't what draws me to the space.

There's a low wall a few feet away from the end of the bed and two steps that lead into a sitting area with two cozy-looking chairs. The giant window takes up most of the wall and overlooks not only the pool, but the entire Phoenix valley. There's even a small balcony.

I'm in love. It's perfect.

"Ahem."

I spin around and see Dad and Justin standing in the doorway, each with two suitcases in hand. My purse is slung over Justin's shoulder.

"Thanks," I say. "You can put them down anywhere."

"Good choice on the room," Dad tells me. "It's our guests' favorite."

"Oh!" My cheeks flush and I try not to look disappointed. "I can take a different one, then."

"Nonsense. This is your house now," he says, and I notice he doesn't make the mistake of calling it my home a second time. "Settle in. We'll have dinner at seven."

I nod and he smiles and walks out. Justin lingers for a second.

"Yeah?" I ask him.

He shrugs and shakes his head. "Nothing," he says. "Just nice to have you around again, Holls."

His old nickname for me sends a wave of nausea pumping through my veins. "Your girlfriend's waiting by the pool."

He studies me for a second, then nods. "She isn't my girlfriend, but yeah, you're probably right. I should get back out there. Let me know if you need anything."

"Close the door behind you."

When the lock clicks firmly into place, I let out a sigh and sink down onto the plush bed that isn't mine and feel tears spring to my eyes.

I don't even have my bed anymore. I just have these four suitcases, my guitar, my backpack and my purse. The bed I've slept in for the last ten years belongs to someone else in eastern Pennsylvania now, sold alongside everything else from our life because my mom isn't going to need the

furniture -- or the house I grew up in after the move --
where she's going with her new husband in Europe.

I wipe frantically at my eyes and dig around in my
suitcase for dry clothes to change into.

No crying. I'm here now.

I can't do much about it.

And I've got to figure out a way to make it work.

CHAPTER TWO

I wake up curled in a small ball on the bed an hour later and almost don't remember where I am or why I'm here, but it comes back to me with a bang like it always does. I glance at the bedside alarm clock. 6:15. That only leaves me with forty-five minutes to get ready for whatever Dad has planned for dinner.

I crack open my door and peek my head out into the hall. Empty. I creep down to Justin's room and tap lightly on his door.

A second later, he opens it and sticks only his head out.

"Oh, it's you," he says, opening the door a little wider.

"Who'd you think it was?"

"Dad. Or Tanya. I'm not used to having you around. What's up?"

"What's dinner tonight? I mean, do I have to dress up?"

He laughs. "We're going out, yeah."

"What are you wearing?"

"Why, you wanna borrow something from my closet?"

I roll my eyes. Maybe Justin hasn't changed so much after all.

"Khakis," he says after a second. "And a button down. No tie or anything. Don't get crazy."

I smile. "Thanks."

He nods and I turn and head back down the hall to root through my suitcase for something suitable. I decide on a flowery sundress, white sweater and flat brown sandals. Nice enough to match Justin's clothes but not so elaborate that I look like I'm trying too hard.

Dad, Tanya and Justin are already waiting in the foyer by the time I reach the stairs, and I instantly feel bad that I'm holding them up.

I'm already an intruder in their house. I don't want to make it worse.

I follow them down another hallway that I haven't taken yet and we come out in a giant five-car garage. Only one of the stalls is empty; the rest house a Jaguar, a BMW, a Range Rover and a Mercedes.

Oh.

We get in the Range Rover and I immediately long for the comfort of my Honda. There's nothing in here -- it may as well be the model unit on a dealer's showroom floor. It doesn't look lived in. No character.

I hate it.

We ride to the restaurant in loud silence as I take in everything about my new town that isn't really new. I used to live here (not in such a fancy house, of course) but it doesn't feel familiar to me. Pennsylvania is what I know even if Arizona was my first home.

Dad doesn't bother parking the Range Rover; he drives straight up to the valet service, which is something I can't ever remember taking advantage of in Pennsylvania. It always seemed silly to me, and it still does as we pile out of the car and he hands his keys to the pimpled teenage guy who looks like he can't wait to get his hands on a car like this.

Risky business, if you ask me, but then again, I'm not the one with the money to throw at a full garage of fancy cars.

We march into the restaurant, every employee seemingly falling over themselves to make sure we don't touch the doors ourselves and we're shown immediately to our table, without so much as a word spoken by any of us.

A far cry from the familiar restaurants back in Pennsylvania where they know me by name and aren't afraid to ask about the last bit of drama they remember hearing about from my last trip in for a burger and curly fries.

I have a feeling I'm not going to be able to find fries like those on the menu tonight.

"What do you think, Holly?" Dad asks once we've been seated and the waiter has placed our napkins on our laps for us. "Nice, isn't it?"

I glance around the restaurant. It isn't very full, but each table has a long white linen tablecloth with one flickering candle on the center. The dim lights and low-hanging chandeliers suggest a place more suited for romance than a family dinner, but Dad is right. It's nice.

It's just not really my thing.

"It's very pretty," I say diplomatically.

Dad smiles, but I don't miss the look on Tanya's face even if she doesn't glance my way. She knows better than Dad does.

"Please, order whatever you like," he says, gesturing to the thick leather menu on the table in front of me. "The steak is always outstanding here."

I flip open the menu. I love steak, and had already been thinking about getting it, but now that he's suggested it, it's lost its appeal. Maybe it's childish, but I just can't stand the idea that he might think I'm giving in to him, that this is some kind of peace offering on my part.

I don't know how he'd get all that from a steak, but it's a chance I'm not willing to take.

I force my eyes away from the different cuts of meat and over to the pasta section. When Justin and I were kids, our parents hated it when we ordered spaghetti and meatballs at restaurants because it was one of the few things they knew how to cook for us at home, but we did it all the time anyway.

I don't see it listed on the fancy menu in front of me, but I know what I'm ordering, anyway.

I close the menu and wait for the rest of the table to figure out what they want. When the waiter appears, Justin asks for lobster, Dad a steak and Tanya a salad.

He turns his attention to me. "For you, miss?"

I smile sweetly at him. He can't be much older than twenty, so I hope this works. "I have a bit of a favor to ask," I say. "I'm hoping you could help me out with something that isn't on the menu. I just really have a craving for spaghetti and meatballs. Can you do that?"

The waiter's face turns from startled to relieved as I finish my request, but Justin starts coughing as he chokes on the water he'd been taking a sip before I placed my order.

"Very well," the waiter says, closing his pad and walking away.

Dad's staring at me with a funny expression and Justin's face is bright red and he's struggling not to laugh as I reach for my glass.

"Spaghetti and meatballs?" Tanya says, and I find it funny that she's the one who chooses to comment on my order considering she's the only one who has no clue what it means. "Interesting choice, Holly."

"It was always a favorite of mine when we went out to eat," I reply smoothly.

"I should've let you order first, Holls," Justin says, winking at me. "I'm jealous."

"So, Holly," Dad cuts in. "Any plans for your first real day in Phoenix tomorrow?"

I nod. "Might as well get started on my job hunt."

Dad looks startled. "Your what?"

"Well, I need to get a job."

"That's preposterous."

I wrinkle my forehead, and glance over at Justin, who suddenly looks like he wishes he could be anywhere else but at this table right now.

"No, it isn't," I say.

"You don't have to *work*, Holly," Dad says with a laugh, like it's cute that the idea even crossed my mind at all. "I have more than enough money."

Justin sucks in a breath and even Tanya has the decency to look uncomfortable.

As for me?

I'm not even sure how to react.

But mostly, I'm just really freakin' angry.

"I don't want your money," I manage to stammer out between gritted teeth.

Dad looks genuinely confused. "But why not? I have plenty of it."

"Because," I say, hands gripping the table. "I somehow made it through the last ten years of my life without needing your money, and that isn't going to change now."

Dad looks stricken, and I'm afraid to look at my brother because, despite everything, I kind of like Justin and don't want him to think I'm attacking him here. This is only between me and my father.

"Ron," Tanya cuts in then as Dad and I stare at one another across the table. "I think if Holly wants to get a job, that's a fine idea. She'll have too much free time on her hands otherwise."

Dad looks over at his wife. "I thought she'd help out with the team," he pouts.

"The what?" I ask, curiosity winning out. As far as I know, my dad hasn't been involved with baseball since he retired from the pros six years ago.

"Your father is coaching a baseball team," Tanya says.

I frown and look at him. "Pro?"

Dad shakes his head. "A summer league for college players. Justin plays for me."

I glance at my brother, who nods. "Oh."

"Yeah," Justin says. "It's a good way for us to keep in shape over the summer. Fun to get to know different players around the country who spend the break in Arizona, too."

I nod. It makes sense.

Even if the thought of baseball has made my skin crawl ever since that one day.

"You need me to do something for that?" I ask Dad even though I have limited interest in helping him out. I really don't want to be involved with anything baseball.

Dad shakes his head. "I could come up with a position for you, I'm sure."

"No, thanks. I'd rather just get a real job."

"You should come to some of our games, though, Holls," Justin says, and I'm glad he's shifting the conversation away from my decision to work. I'm not wild about my father, and I might enjoy antagonizing him over spaghetti, but I don't want to cause a public scene.

"Maybe I will. You guys any good?"

Justin shrugs. "We could be. But it's not that serious. Just a fun league around the state."

"Sounds cool," I say. "I'll have to check it out, I guess."

Dad beams, like this is me suddenly forgiving him and I'm not mad about him trying to buy me off. I try not to sigh.

It's a fight I'll save for another day.

CHAPTER THREE

I look at the keys to my green Honda hanging on the cork board next to the ones for the sleek black BMW sedan that Dad had offered me, but I can't bring myself to take his car even if I know I'll stick out like a sore thumb in my dented little car on the Scottsdale streets. It's still my baby and I can't abandon it like this.

Not for something of his, anyway.

This car is still me, Pennsylvania me. The person I don't want to lose just because I'm not there anymore.

I grab the keys to my Honda and head down to the ridiculous garage where Justin had moved my car after dinner last night despite my protests that I could do it myself.

"It works out just beautifully," Dad had said in the car on the way back to the house. "We have one free garage you can use."

Perfect, indeed.

I jump into the driver's seat and rest my head against the steering wheel, letting out a small sigh of relief. This is the only place in all of Arizona -- the only place for almost 3,000 miles -- that feels like home to me.

The list of jobs that I printed off the Internet is tucked safely in a folder in my purse along with copies of my sparse -- and embarrassing -- resume. Not that it really matters. I've only been out of high school for a month and outside of operating the cash register at the garden store in town, I haven't really done a thing.

But that isn't going to stop me now. I need to find a way to make money even if Dad says I have unlimited access to that shiny black credit card he handed me at dinner last night. I haven't changed my mind about using that.

I won't.

With a dramatic sigh, I shove the key into the engine a little more forcefully than maybe I should but it feels good, like just a little bit of tension seeps out of my shoulders.

I pull the list of jobs out of my bag and enter the first address into my trusty GPS and navigate down the sloped driveway, putting more and more distance between myself and the craziness of the past 24 hours with every roll of my tires.

It only takes me about fifteen minutes to get down to the local gym that's advertising for a few front desk receptionist. I'm pretty sure I can handle swiping ID cards without any past experience. I'm at least good enough for this.

I pull into the parking lot and into a space between a sleek, shiny black Audi and a bright red, two-door BMW convertible with the top down.

Great.

I take a deep breath before pushing open the door to the gym and ask the tall, tanned girl currently behind the desk if I can speak with the manager.

"You got a problem?" she asks, snapping the gum between her lips.

I blink. "N-no, I just want to apply for the desk job opening I saw online."

She slowly scans me from head to toe and smirks. "Sure ya do. I'll go grab him."

I frown as she disappears inside the office behind the desk. She's back a few seconds later with a short, chubby bald guy trailing after her.

"You wanna be my desk girl, eh?" he asks in a heavy New York accent.

"I saw the listing online."

Just like the girl had a few minutes before, he looks me up and down, and I have to fight the urge not to cross my arms over my chest.

"It's a nice idea, cupcake, but I usually like my employees to be in shape."

Now it's my turn to check me out. "I, uh..."

"Yeah, I know, you ain't fat," he says, waving his hand in the air like he's heard it all before. "But that don't mean you're in shape. You ever hear of skinny fat? I think that's what you are."

I open my mouth to protest but he doesn't let me get a word in.

"You ain't got any muscle tone on them arms or legs there. When's the last time you worked out? I can't have somebody that don't work out runnin' my desk. Be like putting out a plate o' glazed Krispy Kremes as a welcome every morning. You get that, right, cupcake? Ain't nothin' personal."

It's stupid and silly and he obviously isn't someone I'd ever want to work for anyway, but I can already feel the lump forming in my throat, and the first threat of tears prickling at the corner of my eyes. I nod once, swallow, refuse to look at anyone and quickly turn and run out.

I don't stop running until I'm safely locked in the familiar comfort of my Honda.

I wipe frantically at my eyes. This is stupid. I shouldn't be upset about it. These people are clearly crazy.

But it doesn't matter.

My first rejection in Arizona doesn't feel good at all, like it's the first sign maybe I made a mistake coming here.

I pick up the red pen I clipped to my job hunting folder last night and angrily scribble over the Carmine's Fitness Emporium listing. On to the next: Gemma's Cafe.

It sounds friendlier than Carmine's, anyway.

Gemma's isn't too far down Scottsdale Road, at least according to my GPS, so I toss the car into reverse and back out the parking spot.

The cafe is in a decent-looking strip mall with a grocery store, bank branch, Chinese restaurant and a few other boutique-y-type stores. There are several outdoor tables behind a black wrought iron fence and a ton of plants in front of Gemma's. White Christmas lights hanging from the leaves of the small potted palms and are wrapped around the fence.

It doesn't, I have to admit, look terrible.

Better than the gym, anyway.

As I walk up past the outdoor tables, I notice a handful of brightly-colored flyers hanging in the windows, all advertising a different local band that'll be playing at the cafe sometime in June. The chalkboard on the sidewalk says that something called JOHNNY AND HIS ROCKETS will be playing at nine o'clock tonight.

I push open the door, the bells jingle and I'm instantly greeted warmly by the girl who looks about my age wiping down the back counter.

"What can I get for you today?" she asks, tossing the rag under the register and washing her hands.

"Actually, I wanted to apply for the waitressing job I saw online?"

"You asking me or telling me?" she says with a smile.

"What?"

"You said that like it was a question," she says. "So I asked you if you're telling me you're here to apply for the job or if you know you're here to apply for the job. Gemma's not gonna hire someone who isn't sure they want to be here."

I'm not sure I want to work at Gemma's, not at all, but I need the money.

"I'm, uh, telling you," I say, and she grins.

"Right answer. When can you start?"

"Now? I mean, now."

"Then you're hired. Grab an apron."

"Are you -- ?"

"Gemma?" she asks. "No. But I'm her granddaughter and we need the help and here you are. So, like I said, grab an apron."

"Um, well, okay. Where can I find one?"

She grins. "Come around back and I'll get you set up. I'm Natalie Melter."

"Oh, right. Holly."

I wander around the counter and display filled with cakes and cookies and pastries and through a door marked 'Employees Only", my job hunting list long forgotten.

Funny. I'm an employee now, I guess.

Natalie meets me on the other side of the door with an apron, which I tie around my waist.

"Okay," she says, nodding as she looks at me. "Good. You already look the part. I have someone coming in two hours from now so you can go home then and we'll figure out a schedule for the rest of the week."

"That seems reasonable."

"Good." Natalie smiles. "First thing I need you to do is clean all the counters out front and wipe down the tables."

I shrug. "Sure." It isn't glamorous, but it's something to do, and it'll keep me busy, and for that, I'm grateful.

Natalie shows me where the mops and rags and cleaning products are kept in the back of the store, and then the bells jingle and we have a customer and she's hurrying out front, leaving me to figure out exactly what I need to use to wipe down all the surfaces.

I stuff a couple of cloth rags into the pockets of my apron and settle on a spray bottle labeled CLEANER. It's either that, floor wash or dish detergent, and while I might not know a whole lot about working in food service, I'm pretty sure I'm right about this.

I wander through the employee door and out into the cafe where there are several people scattered at different tables, most with a coffee or pastry in front of them, all with laptops or tablets.

I begin spraying and wiping the empty tables, when I hear it:

"Holly *Shaw*?"

The voice is so familiar but so full of disbelief that it makes me strangely terrified to look up and see who it is that managed to recognize me just a day after my return.

And when I do, I can't help but frown.

I have no idea who the girl with the long blonde hair and pink sundress is in front of me.

"Yeah," I say. "I'm Holly."

"Omigosh! It's so good to see you again! What are you doing here? You came home and you didn't even *call*?"

Uh oh.

"I've been, uh, busy."

She narrows her eyes. "You have no idea who I am, do you?"

I bite my lip. "Um, no, sorry. It's been a long time since I've been in town."

"It's Natasha." When I don't react, she sighs. "Peterson. Natasha Peterson."

"Natasha...Peterson," I mutter, trying to place the name. It isn't unfamiliar to me, but I can't quite get my memory to reach it, either. I let out a breath. "Sorry. It's just not ringing that bell, you know?"

"From elementary school," she insists. "Mrs. Brewer's class." I squint, trying to take myself back to third grade. I remember Mrs. Brewer and the blow-up beach ball we used to play Around the World with on Friday afternoons if we behaved during the week. I stare at Natasha and her blonde hair and can vaguely picture a little girl with the same curls and big blue eyes whispering to Tina McElroy when Mrs. Brewer wasn't looking.

"Oh," I say, not sure if the memory is actually real or if it's only coming back to me because Natasha expects it to. "Yeah, I think I remember."

She breaks out into a smile. "I knew you would. What are you doing back in town? Summer break?"

"Oh, ah...something like that," I say nonchalantly.

"We should totally hang out sometime!"

I'm not expecting her to say this. "Okay," I hear myself replying without even thinking about it. "I guess we can do that."

I'm not wild about the idea, really, but at least it's something that'll get me out of Dad's house for a couple of hours.

"Really? Great, give me your phone!'

I dig my cell phone out of the back pocket of my jeans and pass it to her. She fiddles with it for a few seconds, then hands it back to me with a wide smile.

"Perfect!" she says. "This'll be so great."

I try to plaster a smile of my own on my face, but it's hard to fake the kind of enthusiasm Natasha has right now. Luckily for me, she doesn't seem to notice.

"Anyway," she goes on. "I have to jet. Great seeing you, Holly!" She leans in and air kisses both of my cheeks. "Talk soon!"

Natasha swings out of the cafe, her expensive shoes clicking against the tile floor as she goes, leaving me standing there with a dirty rag in my hand, wondering if I made a huge mistake by coming here.

"You're friends with her?" Natalie calls to me after her customer leaves.

I stop wiping down the counter and sigh. "Not really."

"Probably should keep it that way."

I go back to cleaning and as I get closer to the tables by the door, I catch sight of the musical posters hanging in the windows once more.

"You guys do live music?" I ask without looking at her.

"We try to," she says. "But it's not that easy to find acts."

I'm surprised. I would've thought they'd have so many applications that they could hold auditions or something.

"Why?" she continues. "Know somebody?"

I bite down on my bottom lip and think about the guitar laying next to my bed, the song notebook beside on the floor.

"No," I say after a minute. "I was just curious."

"You sure?" Natalie asks. I glance up at her and she's looking back at me with raised eyebrows. "You play something, don't you?"

I finish wiping the table, grab the rag and spray bottle, and head back through the employee door. I put them away, then walk out behind the counter to join her.

"Guitar," I say. "And sometimes I sing."

She smiles. "Knew it. Why don't you play here sometime?"

I shake my head. "Nope. No way."

"Why not?"

"I've never done it."

"So?"

"I don't know if I can."

Natalie waves me off. "Please. It'll always be 'don't know' until you actually try it, right?"

"Yeah."

"So find out for sure."

"I don't know...."

She shrugs. "Fine. Just think about it, okay? We're open all next week."

"Okay," I say. "I will."

I think about the guitar resting safely in my bedroom back at Dad's, and wonder if I'll consider it at all.

CHAPTER FOUR

I'm lying on my bed, staring up at the boring beige ceiling, trying to work up the motivation to practice something on the guitar, when a knock on the door rattles me out of my daze. I pick myself up and shuffle over, peeking my head out.

Justin's standing in the hall in his swim trunks and flip-flops.

"Come down to the pool," he says.

"Oh, no, I can't."

He raises an eyebrow. "Why not?"

"I don't want to intrude."

He sighs. "Holly, come on, I told you."

"I know, I know. But I would just feel weird."

"Well, don't," he says. "Get your suit on and come downstairs. I have some friends coming over, too."

"Oh, then I'd definitely rather not -- "

"I'm not gonna take no for an answer," he says, leaning against the door frame and crossing his arms over his chest. "Just so you know."

I let out a sigh. "I'm not going to win, am I?"

He shakes his head. "Nope. Never. Just like when we were little."

I tense up at the thought of some trip down memory lane with him. There's something I definitely don't want to explore. "Okay, okay. I'll meet you down there."

He gives me a big self-satisfied grin before he turns and walks away, whistling to himself, and leaving me to find a bathing suit and gather my thoughts.

I root through my suitcases since I haven't bothered unpacking yet -- I don't know when I'll be ready to do that and really move in -- but I can only come up with two bikinis from back home, and I don't really want to wear either, considering it's been months since I've let the sun really touch my skin.

I lay both of them out on my bed and stare down at them -- one is purple with big white polka dots, the other red and stringy -- before remembering that I'm just going downstairs to meet my brother and I don't care about impressing his friends, especially if they're all like that girl from yesterday, so it doesn't really matter what I wear.

I grab the red one after examining the pulls on the butt of the purple bottoms and change into it quickly. I toss a short blue cotton dress over my head as a makeshift cover-up and jam my feet into a pair of jeweled sandals. A quick head-to-toe application of sunscreen, lip balm and a messy ponytail later, and I grab my headphones and book, and head down to the pool I'm supposed to consider my own.

Fat chance.

I walk out onto the deck and see Justin coming out of the pool house with a stack of dry towels in his arms as I walk over to an empty lawn chair.

"Here." Justin tosses two burnt orange towels down onto the lounger. "Use these."

"Thanks."

I spread out my towels, lower the back of the chair to a sleeping position and flop down, pulling my sunglasses over my eyes, and let the hot desert sun soak into my pale Pennsylvania skin.

My feet bop in time to the beat of the song playing over my headphones, but I barely hear it. I'm slowly losing track of this world as the heat warms my bones. It's perfect right here and now, with the slight breeze rustling through the palm trees. All my cares, as they say, are slipping away, and it's getting easier and easier to forget the craziness of the last year of my life.

And that's when I hear the shouts distant through the headphones. My eyelids flutter a few times before popping wide open at the shrill scream of a girl.

Four guys and two girls stand on the deck on the other side of the pool with Justin, all of them talking at once, and all of them ruining my peaceful state.

I'm grateful right now for the privacy my sunglasses offer; I can be a total creep on them without having them realize I'm staring.

I don't recognize anyone, not that I would even if I had known them when I was little and lived out here. Justin's girl from the other day isn't with them, and two of the guys have their tanned, shirtless backs to me. The ones that I can see aren't particularly cute, either. I shrug and hope they aren't going to be too loud, or else me coming down the pool was a bad idea like I'd originally thought it was.

I close my eyes, hoping to get back to that happy place I'd found just a few minutes ago.

But it isn't long before the shouts and splashes and cries of excitement seep into my ears and filter in even with the headphones. I let out a sigh and prop myself up on my elbows.

Two of the guys, both girls and my brother are treading water in the deep end of the pool near the mouth of the rock slide. I'm not sure why they're hanging out in the eight-foot waters or what happened to the others, but I don't want to get caught staring or roped into joining them.

I flip over onto my back so I'm forced to look away and can focus on tuning out the rest of the currently very obnoxious world.

The next thing I know, I feel a light mist covering my back and I whip my head around and almost scream.

Standing above me with a spray bottle of sunscreen is none other than the complete and total jackass from the black pick-up truck my first night in town.

"What the hell are you doing here?" I demand, flipping over, ripping the earbuds out of my ears and instinctively wrapping the towel around my exposed body as tightly as I can.

He blinks twice. "Do I know you?"

"Yeah, you know me," I snap. "You're the asshole who likes to race your car down heavily trafficked roads in the middle of the day."

"Heavily trafficked roads?" He grins and shakes his head. "It's too nice of a summer day for such big words."

I glare at him. "What are you doing in my yard?"

"Your yard?"

"My dad's yard, whatever," I say, surprising myself at how willing I am to take ownership of this place -- and my father -- right now. "Doesn't change the question."

"I hang out here from time to time when Justin invites me," he says.

"You know him?"

He looks at me like I'm dumb. "Uh, yeah. I'm here all the time, but I've never seen you around. What's up with that?"

"I'm new in town."

He raises an eyebrow.

"And you're here to stay?"

"Something like that."

"Wait," he says, squinting like his mind is working in overdrive. It probably is. "And how do you know Justin again?"

"He's my brother."

The guy blinks rapidly. "You're Justin's sister?"

"She's my little sister," Justin pipes up. He's sitting on the edge of the pool not far from us, legs dangling in the water, clearly listening in to the conversation.

"Dude, I didn't know you had a sister."

I refuse to meet Justin's eyes but I can feel his on me now. "Well, I do. Always have."

"Sweet." The guy turns his attention back to me. "I'm Doan Riley."

I glare at him. "You're still an asshole."

Justin laughs. "You know him?"

"Yeah," I say, keeping my eyes firmly planted on Doan. "Do you?"

It's a pointed question and I'm not sure Justin will pick up on it, but he shoots me a knowing grin.

"That's why I keep him around."

"Interesting judge of character, big bro."

"I didn't say I want to be him, Holls."

"Holls?" Doan looks at me. "That your name?"

"No."

"It's Holly," Justin says, and I shoot him a dirty look.

"Anyway," I say. "What the heck is up with the sunscreen?"

Doan glances down at the bottle of lotion in his hand. "Oh, I'm big on sunblock," he says. "My brother got deployed to Iraq and all he ever talked about was how important SPF was out there. I didn't know if you were sleeping and had lotion on your back. It's just a spray bottle. I didn't touch you."

I stare at him for a second, surprised by the softness in his voice. "Oh," I say, taken aback. "Okay. Um, thanks."

"He's not kidding," Justin adds. "Dude's constantly after us to wear sunblock. Katie hates him for it."

Doan looks at me, nods and smiles. "Nothing devious here, I promise."

It still doesn't change what I think about him, but even I have to admit it's nice.

"Got it." I don't know what else to say.

"Okay," Doan says, and I don't miss how awkward this conversation has become since I brought up the sunscreen thing. "You coming swimming with us?"

"Not right now."

"Come on, you should."

I shake my head. "I'm good out here."

He shrugs. "Suit yourself."

I lean against the back of the lawn chair as Doan tosses the sunscreen bottle onto the table and runs for the stairs to the water slide. My sunglasses are back in place and I'm comfortable taking in the scene in front of me again.

Doan comes flying down the slide, slamming into the water with a splash that soaks the deck and almost reaches my chair.

He pops up out of the water and swims over to the ledge that runs around the side and hoists himself onto it, running a hand through his short dirty blonde hair. The sun catches the silver metal dog tags hanging around his neck. I wonder if they belong to his brother, and why Doan wears them now.

I don't miss the way his tan washboard abs have no pockets of extra fat anywhere as he sits, and how his biceps flex with every movement of his hand. I've always loved that ripple of the vein that runs down a guy's arm when he has particularly strong definition in his muscles there. My mouth runs dry when I catch sight of Doan's, and I quickly look away.

I can't stand him, but I'm not blind. I can't help it if I notice these things, right?

CHAPTER FIVE

"Coming out to the diamond today?"

Justin wanders into the kitchen dressed in shorts and a T-shirt and rests his dusty baseball glove on the counter next to my bowl of cereal.

I wrinkle my nose and look up at him. "Really?"

"What? Baseball that offensive to you, Holls?"

"Not that."

He follows my gaze to his glove. "That bother you?"

"It's gross."

"Sorry." He reaches over and picks it up. "Not used to living with a girl."

I raise an eyebrow. "What do you consider Tanya?"

"She doesn't count."

I decide not to press him for more information about Dad's wife. "Oh. Well, I think I'll skip it," I say, knowing that it means extra togetherness with Dad around, which is exactly what I'm trying to avoid if I can help it.

"Staying home?" Tanya comes sweeping into the kitchen in a wash of perfume and heels and red lipstick. "It's a beautiful day. Come with me to the spa."

Justin coughs and puts his mitt over his mouth.

"The spa?" I repeat.

Tanya digs around in her expensive-looking designer handbag and doesn't look at me. "Yes, of course. I have an appointment. Facial, massage, manicure, the works. It's simply divine. You must come."

"Actually, Tanya, thanks, but I think I'm going to head to practice with Justin and Dad."

She barely even blinks. "Suit yourself," she says like it doesn't bother her at all that I'm not going.

Tanya walks out of the kitchen like Justin and I aren't even there, and we both let out a breath when she's gone.

He's grinning at me. "Baseball it is!"

I sigh. "Baseball it is."

"Go get dressed," he says, and I glance down at my pajamas. "I'll meet you in the garage."

***

Justin pulls his BMW into a small gravel parking lot in front of what looks like a big patch of grass and some dirt. I'd offered to drive my Honda, but he'd just looked at me and laughed.

A handful of guys are already out in the grass tossing around a baseball. Justin gets out of the car, and I follow him a few steps behind. I scan the field for my father, but I don't see him yet.

I start wandering over to the metal bleachers behind a chain-link fence where I figure I'll sit and watch practice and soak up more of the sunshine. My legs had gotten a nice bit of color yesterday by the pool, but I'm still as pale as a ghost by Arizona standards.

I'm scrolling through my phone when I hear the fence rattle. I look up and see a ball lying on the grass next to it as a guy dressed in basketball shorts jogs over to it.

I glance back down at my phone, not interested in making small talk.

"I hope you've got sunblock on."

I snap my head back up, and there's Doan, grinning at me from beneath a Phoenix Coyotes baseball hat. He's tossing the stray baseball back and forth between his hand and glove.

I smile even though nothing about him makes me happy. I reach into the bag by my feet, pull out my bottle of sunscreen and wave it at him.

"Here you go."

"Good job, lady. Sun's hot today."

"Isn't it hot everyday?"

He laughs. "You make a good point."

"Soon enough you'll learn not to sound surprised about that."

Doan raises an eyebrow. "Oh, yeah?"

"So this is practice?" I ask, changing the subject.

He blinks once. "Oh. Uh, we didn't start yet."

"I didn't know you were on this team."

He wiggles his eyebrow at me. "Disappointed to see me here? I'm a pitcher at the University of Arizona."

I roll my eyes. "You're not exactly my favorite person."

Doan places a hand over his heart. "You're killing me, Holly. I don't know what I did to deserve this."

"Yeah, you do."

He sighs. "Come on, I didn't mean anything by it. I was just having some fun."

"Fun that could have killed someone." I shake my head. "It isn't a game, Doan. You can't gamble with people's lives just because you're bored."

He stares at me for a few beats. "I wasn't gambling with -- it's not because I'm -- you know what? Forget it. I can't explain it to someone like you, anyway."

"That's because there is no explanation."

"Let it go, Holly."

I let out a long, bitter laugh. "I'm not going to do that. What you did was so incredibly stupid and it makes me really mad. Sorry if you don't wanna hear it, but I'm gonna tell you what I think."

"I know!" he snaps. "Okay? I know. It's stupid. But that doesn't change anything."

"Change anything about what?"

"What I did. Why I did it. All of it. Nothing changes anyway," he says. "So you can quit it with the lectures. You're wasting your time. And mine."

I stare at him, eyes narrowed, mouth open, stunned he has the gall to yell at me about what he did.

"Fine," I say. "If you want to get yourself killed, that isn't my problem."

Something flashes in his eyes, and I have no idea what it is, but it's there just long enough to startle me.

"You're right," he hisses. "It isn't your problem. So stop trying to make it one."

I look at him, realizing I'm breathing a little bit heavier than normal, my heart thumping against my chest as we stare at one another.

"Doan, I -- "

"Don't, Holly. Just...don't. I have to get back to practice."

I don't get a chance to say anything as he turns and jogs away from me. I don't even know what I'd want to tell him, if I could tell him anything, or why this bothers me so much, but there's a thick cement brick in my stomach. This car-racing thing, it isn't just fun, stupid recklessness. There's something else there.

And for some reason, I'm not going to be able to let it go until I figure out what it is.

***

Dad's been at the field for almost two hours now, and I can't stop watching the practice even though I'd thought I had no interest in it as anything other than a reason to escape girls' day with Tanya.

My brother is pretty good at baseball -- all of the guys are -- but my eyes keep wandering over to Doan as he works on the pitcher's mound.

He's good at what he does, but I'm not watching him so I can suggest improvements for his curveball.

I don't really know why I can't take my eyes off of him because if I could draw up the exact opposite of what I want in a guy, Doan's it.

Except for the whole drool-inducing abs and gorgeous eyes and annoyingly sexy smile, but there's not much I can do about that. Besides, his personality more than ruins any bonus he earns from his time in the gym.

"Alright!" Dad yells out, clapping his hands. "That'll do for today, gentlemen. Nice practice."

The guys all jog over to the bleachers where I'm sitting to gather their things and head to their cars.

"We're gonna grab some pizza," Justin says to me as I stand and pick up my bag. My stomach growls as soon as he mentions food. "You in?"

I catch sight of Doan climbing into the front seat of his black pick-up truck, the sun reflecting off of the metal dog tags hanging around his neck, and suddenly I want to tell Justin no thanks, but my stomach rumbles again and he laughs.

"I'll take that as a yes," he says, and I frown. "Besides, you've gotta ride home with Dad if you don't come. He'll love that."

I sigh and open the passenger side door of his car, and he smiles.

"Good choice."

"I didn't know Doan was on the team," I say once we pull out of the parking lot and into traffic. His truck is just a few cars in front of ours and I notice an Arizona Wildcats baseball decal on the back window for the first time.

Justin glances over at me. "Yeah, he is. He's one of the best pitchers in the state. I saw you talking to him before."

"He's kind of a jerk."

"Yeah, he is. But cut him some slack. He has his reasons."

I shake my head. "Nothing excuses him."

Don't be so judgmental."

I glare at my brother, mouth hanging open. "How can you say that? Do you even know what he did?"

"I can guess," Justin says. "But it doesn't matter. I know his story."

"Okay, so what is it?"

"Not my story to tell, Holls."

"Well, then, I don't know how you expect me to be okay with him."

Justin sighs. "I was hoping you could take my word for it. He'll tell you when he's ready to, if he ever decides that's something he wants. It isn't up to me."

"Then why mention it at all?"

He shrugs. "Doan's my friend and I know there's a solid guy in there most times. Was just hoping you'd trust me."

I shake my head, thinking of the car race down the busy street the other day, the squeal of the tires, the smell of the burning rubber, the cloud of smoke, and all the innocent lives they'd put it danger.

"Whatever."

Justin lets out a sigh, and we drive the rest of the way to the restaurant in silence. I'm hoping that Doan will have just decided to go home and his pick-up won't be in the parking lot, but Justin pulls into a space right next to the truck.

Great.

We're the last to arrive and the hostess walks us over to a long table in the middle of the place. There are only two seats left; one, naturally, is right next to Doan.

He grins at me -- an obnoxious, toothy, arrogant grin -- when I glance at him, and I frown. I'm grateful that Justin's walking in front of me. He knows how I feel about Doan; there's no way I'll have to be the one to sit next to him.

But then Justin drops into the seat next to the curly red-haired guy, leaving the only empty chair next to Doan, and my heart stutters and a pit forms in my stomach and mostly I just want to smack my brother across the face.

I narrow my eyes as I flop down into the chair.

Hey Holls," Doan says cheerfully, like he wasn't just yelling at me a few hours ago.

I glance at him out of the corner of my eye. "Hi," I mutter. "Don't call me Holls."

Justin nudges me with his foot under the table, and that's when I realize he did this on purpose. He wants me to sit next to Doan. Is he crazy? I press my sandal down onto his sneaker as hard as I can, and I smile when I hear him mutter an obscenity under his breath.

Good.

Serves him right.

"So, pizza," says one of the guys sitting at the other end of the table. "I'm thinking four of them. Pick 'em like we usually do."

I've always been fussy about my pizza toppings so this guy's announcement sends me into a moment of panic.

"How do you usually pick them?" I whisper to Justin.

"There are twelve of us tonight, so three of us will decide on a pie for the whole table and then we wind up with four different pizzas with whatever on them. It's sweet."

"You don't get weird things on them, do you?"

He shrugs. "Sometimes."

"You know I can only have pepperoni."

"Me too," Doan says, and I glance at him over my shoulder with a scowl on my face. "But I usually get sucked into eating something gross on my pizza here."

"That's the worst," I say politely.

"I'll split pepperoni with you," he offers.

"That's okay."

"You're gonna be picking anchovies and spinach and pineapples off your slices if you don't."

I let out a small sigh. It's just pizza, right?

"Fine, fine."

He grins at me like he's won some kind of battle. "Awesome."

We all place our orders for the different pizzas and then the guys fall into smaller conversations, most of them about baseball. Justin's talking to the two guys across the table from him, while Doan's deep into a discussion with the guys on his other side.

That leaves me staring awkwardly at the jars of peppers and Parmesan cheese in the middle of the table.

I'm examining my cuticles and deciding that I need to put on a fresh coat of pink nail polish after I get home later when Doan turns in his seat to face me.

I glance up at him and raise an eyebrow. "Yeah?"

"How'd you end up here?"

"Justin asked if I was hungry."

He grins and shakes his head. "Not what I meant."

"I know."

"Are you always such a smart ass?"

"When it benefits me."

"How does it benefit you now?"

"I don't really like you."

He lays his right hand over his heart and sticks out his bottom lip. "You're killing me, Holls." I open my mouth to protest when he smiles. "I know, I know. Don't call you Holls. I got it."

I'm not sure I like that he already knows exactly what I'm going to say before I say it.

"Yeah," I tell him. "So stop."

He laughs. "So are you going to answer my question?"

"I didn't have much of a choice."

"You always have a choice."

"I wasn't going to move to Canada."

Doan smiles. "It was Arizona or Canada? Okay, maybe you didn't have a choice after all."

I laugh despite myself. "Exactly."

"Where were you before?"

"Pennsylvania."

"And you're complaining about coming here? I thought you were gonna say Hawaii or Florida or something. But Pennsylvania? Is there even anything there?"

I shrug. "It's home."

"Home can be anywhere you want it to be."

"Not here," I tell him, and I glance down at my hands. I still don't like him, but I feel oddly comfortable talking about all of this with him. Maybe it's just because my only alternative is going back to examining my nails while I sit around in awkward silence. "My mom got remarried last month. To an Italian count. She lives in Sicily now."

"You couldn't go with her?"

"I could have, but I didn't want to move to my grandmother's house in Toronto," I say. "You think I would've been okay going to Italy?"

"Good point."

"Yeah. So my father offered me a room while I get my life together and here I am."

"But you don't want to be here."

I shake my head. "I don't know what I want."

"What do you do? High school? College?"

"I just graduated from high school. I'm not sure if college is in the cards for me, though." I don't look at him when I say this; I've seen way too many stares of shock and pity whenever it's come up before.

"Didn't apply?"

"No, I did. I got into a couple of places. Even Arizona State because my mom essentially made me apply there," I say. "I just don't know if I'm gonna go."

"What else would you do?"

I glare at him. "I'll figure it out."

He holds up his hands. "Hey, don't shoot," he says. "I'm just asking."

I sigh. "I know. Touchy subject."

"I bet."

"Enough about me," I say, not liking where this conversation has ended up. "What's your story?"

A storm cloud passes over his face and stays just long enough for me to notice it and wonder why I struck a nerve.

"I don't really have one."

"That isn't what Justin said."

"Justin should keep his mouth shut," Doan grumbles, and I notice his hands have balled up into white-knuckled fists at his side.

"He didn't tell me anything," I say quickly. "Nevermind."

At that moment, four waiters walk over with the different pizzas, and I've never been so grateful to see the food arrive in my life. I hadn't meant to upset him, but I guess Justin's right.

Doan definitely has a story, and it isn't an easy one.

But that just makes me want to hear it even more.

CHAPTER SIX

I'm up in my bedroom later the next night, guitar in my lap, song notebook open on the bed next to me.

I know I'm not going to play at Gemma's or anything, but thinking about it made me realize just how much I'd let music go from my life, and how badly I want it back.

I flip through my notebook -- I've only come up with five original songs, and they're all finished and I like them okay, but there's one song on the very last page that I've been trying to write for months, maybe even years. I don't remember how long it's been.

And it still isn't working the way I want it to.

Probably because it doesn't have an ending, and I can't find the right one.

I read over what I have written already for it and let out a sigh. I scribble the first verse onto a fresh sheet of paper, then tear the old page from my notebook, crumple it into a ball and launch it across the room at my trashcan where it hits the rim and falls harmlessly to the carpet.

I smirk. Fitting.

I flip back a few pages to the first song I ever wrote and pick up my guitar, strumming the opening chords and begin to sing.

I'm almost to the chorus when I hear a knock at my door. I ignore it and keep singing when it sounds again, louder and more persistent this time. With a groan, I put my guitar down on the bed and walk over to the door, expecting to see Dad or Justin standing there, wanting me to come down to the pool again.

Instead, I jump back immediately as Doan leans against the door frame, arms crossed over his bare chest. He's wearing just a pair of bright blue swim trunks and flip flops.

"I didn't know you were a singer," he says.

I swallow hard. He must've just come out of the pool; there are still some water droplets clinging to the muscles on his tanned arms and pecs.

"Uh," I say, shaking my head, trying to regain my composure. Doan, of all people, isn't going to affect me. "You don't know anything about me."

He smirks. "Well, now, that isn't true. I know you don't want to live in Arizona, don't really like your dad and that you're pretty cute when you're all riled up around me."

My nostrils flare. Justin always used to say that was a dead giveaway that I'm either about to let someone have it, or lie.

I'm not sure which one is in play right now with Doan.

"You don't rile me up," I say.

Lying it is.

Doan raises his eyebrows. "Sure thing, Holls. You sound good."

I feel my cheeks grow warm, and I hate my body for betraying me like this. I don't care what Doan Riley thinks about anything that has to do with me.

"Thank you." My voice is calm and cool.

He smiles and shakes his head. "I really don't get it. Why do you hate me so much? I'm not a terrible guy. Most people even think I'm fun."

"If you still don't understand it, you never will. And I'm not most people."

"I know," he says. "Believe me, I know."

"I really should get back to the guitar."

"Do you play in front of people?" he asks.

"No."

"Why not?"

I shrug. "Just never had the chance."

"No, I don't believe that. You can always find the opportunity you're looking for if it's what you really want."

"What are you, some kind of book of proverbs?"

"What?" His forehead creases.

"First, you tell me over pizza that we always have a choice, and now you come out with this line about opportunity?" I raise an eyebrow and fold my arms across my chest.

He grins. "I guess you could say that I'm chock full of life's little wisdoms."

"I don't think that's what you're full of," I mutter under my breath, but he only laughs.

"I'm gonna wear you down, Holly," he tells me. "It's just a matter of time, you know that, right?"

"Wear me down to what, exactly?"

He shrugs. "I'll settle for you being a normal person that can have a conversation without looking for new ways to insult me."

"Why would you want that?"

He laughs. "I think you're interesting. And I think there's a lot more to you than you let on."

"Funny you should say that," I shoot back. "Because I'm pretty sure I'm not the only one."

"Drop it," he says.

"What, so I'm just supposed to tell you everything about me, but you can't tell me about you?"

"I didn't say I want you to tell me everything."

I roll my eyes. "Semantics."

"No," he says. "Not at all. I think there are certain things we all want to keep hidden for whatever reason, and

I don't think there's anything wrong with that. We don't have to share everything with everyone."

I'm not sure what to say to that. I don't think he's wrong.

"Come down to the pool," he says after my pause stretches to awkward heights.

I shake my head. "No, I'm good up here. Gotta work on the music."

"Okay, well, the whole reason I came up to find you was just to give you a head's up, anyway."

"About what?"

"I heard your dad talking to your stepmom downstairs when I was grabbing a Bud Light," he says, and my stomach immediately twists. "He's gonna ask you to play for the team."

"The what?"

"You know, the baseball team." Doan gives me a funny look. "The one he coaches."

I take a step back from him. "Why would he ask me that?"

Doan shrugs. "I don't know. If I had to guess, it's so he can spend more time with you."

I let out a breath. "Great."

"I know I don't know the whole story there," Doan says, looking me straight in the eyes. "Or even the beginning of it. But if I were you, I'd do it. There's never enough time with your family."

I open my mouth to respond, but he shakes his head.

"Just trust me on that one, okay, Holly? No matter what, you can always forgive family. I understand better than you think."

And with one last look at me, Doan gives me a strange little half-smile behind his suddenly sad eyes before he claps his hand against the door frame and turns to walk down the hall.

I lean up against the door and watch him walk away, my eyes drawn to the ripples of the muscles in his back, but I'm not really seeing him.

I can't stop wondering about what he's talking about.

CHAPTER SEVEN

I'm sitting outside on the back porch later that night under the covered patio with a bowl of spaghetti and meatballs when the sliding door opens and Dad steps out onto the deck and glances over at me.

"Hey kiddo," he says, pulling the door shut. "Mind if I join you?"

I look down into my pasta bowl. "No, go ahead."

He walks over and drops into the seat across from me. "Beautiful out tonight, isn't it?"

"Yeah, it is."

"Did you have a good time at practice the other day? It was nice seeing you there," he says, and I close my eyes. This is it. Doan apparently hadn't been kidding like I'd hoped he was.

"It was cool to see."

He nods. "Good. Listen, Holly, I was thinking about something. It would be really great if you joined the team. We're a little thin at third base and could use the extra body. It'd mean a lot to me if you would do it."

I suck in a deep breath and slowly let the air rush out of my body. I really, really don't want to do this. More time with Dad, more time with Doan. I'm not interested in having either.

And then there are the memories to think about. So many memories, so many days, so many nights, weeks, months, years; it'll all come back. I'm not ready for that, can't handle any of it. It isn't time.

I'm about to say no when I glance up at Dad.

"Okay," I find myself saying, and even though I'm not exactly wild about him or what he's asking me to do, the smile on his face when I agree is almost worth the irritation that being on the baseball team will bring.

My answer surprises me; I can't quite believe that word came out of my mouth. But maybe, something in me knows that all isn't quite lost after all.

"You can quit your job down at that cafe, too," Dad says.

I shake my head. "No, I don't want to do that. I like it there."

He looks surprised but recovers quickly. "Okay. Okay, sure. Up to you."

"When does this start?"

"We have a week until our first game," he says. "That's when you'll need to be sharp again."

I nod. "Sounds good."

Dad beams. "I'm glad you're doing this, Holly."

"Uh, yeah. So am I."

"And I'm glad you're home."

I swallow hard; I'm not ready for this. It's one thing to lie about being happy about joining a baseball team and quite another to give my father false hope that maybe I'm ready to forget it all and go back to how things used to be.

Dad looks at me for a few seconds, waiting for me to say something -- anything -- but I don't. I can't. His face flushes, then he nods.

"Don't worry about it, kiddo," he says. "I'll let Justin know you said yes. Enjoy the rest of your...ah, spaghetti and meatballs."

I grimace as Dad springs out of his chair and into the house. I hadn't been trying to take another dig at him with my favorite dinner this time, and I feel kind of bad that he thinks I am.

I let out a breath and stare out over the lit-up pool and at the lights dotting the crisp, clear Arizona night sky.

Dad had been right about one thing.

It really is pretty here.

I bring my fork up to my mouth, but I realize I'm no longer hungry. Agreeing to play baseball isn't settling well with me, and I have no idea what came over me and possessed me to agree to do it.

But I have a sneaking -- and sinking -- suspicion that Doan's little comment about families earlier may have subconsciously guilted me into saying yes, and for that, I make a mental note that I owe him a swift kick to the shins.

I sigh and pick up my bowl and head into the kitchen. If there's anyone out here that I don't want sticking his nose into my business, it's Doan Riley.

CHAPTER EIGHT

I'd gotten a text from Natasha late last night as I'd laid in bed, trying to fall asleep but having no luck. Visions of baseball and Doan and Dad haunted me each time I tried to close my eyes. Natasha had asked me to meet her at a bar in Old Town Scottsdale, but I'd told her there was no chance of me getting out of bed for that.

But somehow she'd managed to convince me to agree to go out tonight even though I don't get off my shift at Gemma's until ten because we've got a local band coming in to play at eight.

But by the time I get to work, I've already texted her and let her know that I think I'm going to be too tired to go out again.

"Natasha Peterson?" Natalie wrinkles her nose as she wipes crumbs off the counter. "I don't know why you'd say yes to doing *anything* with that girl."

I shrug. "She asked and I don't have any other plans."

"So all I have to do is ask you to jump off the North Rim of the Grand Canyon, and you will?"

"Point taken."

"Natasha is bad news."

"I need to meet people."

"You met me!"

"Okay, fine. Let's go out and do something after close then."

She presses her lips together. "Can't. My boyfriend's in town tonight."

"Long distance?"

"Yeah. He's a pro hockey player out in LA usually but he's training in Europe for the month of June. He's got a week off and this is his last night here."

"A pro hockey player? Well, look at you."

She blushes and smiles. "I know. I'm lucky but not because of his job."

I feel a surprising -- and unfamiliar -- twinge of jealousy.

"How long have you guys been together?"

"Almost a year now. I met him when I lived in Wisconsin."

"Good for you guys," I tell her. "But I still need to meet people."

She sighs. "Yeah, I know. I just wish Natasha wasn't involved, that's all."

"What's so bad about her anyway?"

"Better for you to see for yourself," Natalie says, tossing the dirty rag into a bucket beneath the counter.

"Maybe another time," I reply.

The band has just come back inside from their smoke break, ready to play the last hour until the cafe closes.

"You know, we're still free all of next week," she says. "You should do it."

I shake my head and smile. "I don't know what you're talking about."

"Holly, it's a Friday night. Look around. There are ten people in here. What do you think it'll be like if you try it out on a Wednesday?"

"Terrifying."

Natalie sighs as the strum of the acoustic guitar fills the small cafe. "You're making a mistake."

"Maybe," I say with a shrug. "But it's my mistake to make."

"If you say so. Look, all I'm trying to tell you is that I know plenty about taking a chance and doing something you don't think that you can," she says. "My entire hockey career is pretty much defined by exactly that. Sometimes it's better to do something even if you don't think you're ready for it. Most of the time, you just don't realize that you are."

She walks into the back before I can respond, leaving me alone out front. I lean up against the counter while we don't have any customers and watch the band.

They aren't very good. The guitar needs a solid tuning and the lead singer isn't quite in the same key as everybody else, but they look like there's nowhere else they want to be, and there's potential there.

If they can get up there and do it....

Well, maybe Natalie's right.

Maybe I ought to give it a shot after all.

And if I stink, who's going to know, anyway? The handful of customers at Gemma's? So what?

I lock eyes with the lead singer and he looks so happy up there on stage, belting out his music, his lyrics, his chords, that I suddenly know what I have to do.

I walk into the back to find Natalie, who's sitting in front of the computer at the small desk opposite the walk-in freezer.

"I'll do it."

She glances up at me and smiles. "Good," she says. "Because you're working Tuesday and it's open mic night and I already put you down for it."

"How'd you know I'd decide to do it?"

She shrugs. "Music seems like something that you love," she says simply. "And when you love something, it's pretty hard to stay away."

CHAPTER NINE

I'm bleary-eyed and rubbing sleep out of the
corner of my eyes when I stumble into the hallway the next
morning. I'm still tired from my late night up thinking
about music and baseball and Dad and Doan, though I have
no idea what to make of any of it.

I push all the thoughts out of my head as my body
screams for a hot shower. I'm just about to walk into the
bathroom when the door opens and I collide with the bare

chest of none other than the one person I'm trying to force out of my mind.

But suddenly, I'm not nearly so out of it.

I take a step back -- though it's not nearly as fast as it should be -- and glance up at him. He's looking back down at me with a smile and raised eyebrows.

"Well good morning to you, Holly," he says, the cocky arrogance back in his voice. "I didn't know we'd made so much progress in our relationship that we were at this stage already, but don't think I'm complaining."

"What are you <u>doing</u> here?" I pull the towel as tightly around my body as I can.

He shakes his head. "Your brother and I went and grabbed some drinks at the bar down the street. I stay over from time to time when Justin and I have too many brews. Ron doesn't want me driving."

"Can't imagine why," I mutter. "You're a menace."

He grins, his teeth still impossibly white, his face still infuriatingly cute.

"Oh, come on, I thought we got past all that already," he says as though I'm wounding him with my words.

"Yeah, right."

"Holls, you're killin' me."

"Can I get in the bathroom please?" I ask. I'm not sure why I'm out here trying to pick a fight with him, but something in me isn't in the mood to deal with him this early in the morning.

"Oh, by all means," he replies. "Don't let me hold you up." He slips past me and walks down the hall.

I'm glaring at his retreating back as he pushes open the door to the guest bedroom.

"By the way," he says, sticking his head out into the hall and smirking. "You wear that towel well, Holls. Real well. Could give a guy some ideas in that thing."

My mouth drops open, heart beating faster, cheeks burning red almost instantly. He's looking me up and down, and my palms are prickling with sweat under his stare.

What a complete and utter tool.

Justin's bedroom door creaks open. "Holly, what are you doing standing out here? I thought I heard your voice."

"Yeah, you did," I snap. "I ran into that asshole friend of yours."

His forehead creases. "Doan? He's a good dude."

"Yeah, right."

"I thought you were going to give him a chance."

"Fat chance. Too bad he can't keep the jerk hidden for longer than a couple of hours."

Justin looks at me and shakes his head. "You're blind sometimes, you know that, Holly?"

I open my mouth to respond but my brother's already back in his room with his door shut.

"I am not," I say even though there's no one here to listen.

And it's true.

I can see Doan Riley -- and who he is -- with perfect vision.

And I know that he isn't someone I want in my life.

CHAPTER TEN

I park my green Honda in front of Gemma's on Tuesday night, close my eyes and take a deep breath. My guitar and song notebook rest on the backseat, and when I catch sight of them in the rearview mirror, the knot in my stomach tightens. This is really happening.

My first gig.

My first performance in front of someone that isn't my mother. But no, this isn't nerve-wracking at all.

I've always loved music and singing and my guitar, but I've never loved sharing it with others, and I don't know why that is.

But I have a feeling I might be about to find out.

I hop out of the car and pull my things out of the backseat before I walk into Gemma's. Natalie already stands behind the counter and she grins when she sees me come in.

"Hey there, songbird," she says. "You ready for tonight?"

There are only two people in the cafe right now with just half an hour left until the open mic night starts, and I hope it doesn't get much more crowded than this. I can deal with it like it is now.

I let out a deep breath. "I'm closer to chickening out than I am to ready," I admit. "But don't worry, I'm not gonna bail on you. I even brought my guitar."

Natalie smiles. "Good. Stick it in the back and then you can stock all the paper goods. Might as well make yourself useful until you play, right?"

"I'm still on the clock," I say with a grin as I push through the employees only door and drop my guitar and notebook down next to the computer desk. I grab an apron and head back to the front of the cafe armed with napkins and straws and sugar packets.

"So," Natalie says when I come back out. "How's hanging out with Natasha going?"

I smirk. "I've made friends. I don't need Natasha."

She smiles and nods. "Good choice."

As I'm pulling the napkins out from under the cabinet, an acne-ridden guy with long black hair walks up to the counter. He's dressed in dark pants and a neon hot pink T-shirt. He's carrying a worn guitar case and has a spiral school notebook tucked under his left arm.

"I, um, I think I'm supposed to perform here tonight," he says to me in a deep baritone that sounds misplaced coming out of someone who looks the way he does.

I glance over at Natalie's list of people signed up to play. "Adam?"

He nods, wipes his right palm off on the thigh of his pants and extends his hand to me.

I shake it with a smile. "Holly," I tell him. "Looks like you're set to go first. You can go up on the stage and get everything ready if you want."

"Sweet. Thanks. You playing tonight?" he asks.

My eyes widen. "Me?"

Adam gives me a strange look. "Yeah, you."

I shrug. "Maybe. I'm thinking about it." I take in a deep breath. "Yeah, I'm gonna play."

He grins. "Your first time, huh?"

I nod. "That obvious?"

"Yep," he says. "But who cares? I think it's great you're finally gonna do it. Good luck."

He turns and walks away with a newfound bounce in his step that I hadn't noticed when he first came in. I watch him as he carefully sets his guitar case down on the stage. Two other guys join him a minute later, and their excitement is palpable as they talk animatedly with each other, hands waving, smiles widening, eyes brightening.

Exactly the way it should be when you're about to do something you love.

I feel a pang of something -- I'm not sure what -- flutter through me as I take in their preparations.

I can do all of this. I know I can. So I'm not sure why it's so hard for me to accept that maybe this is the right move. I'm not even really sure what's trying to hold me back at this point and I suddenly have the overwhelming urge to run up onto the stage, grab the acoustic guitar out of Adam's hands and belt out my favorite song to the handful of people in attendance.

I take a deep breath. It's better than I felt about this five minutes ago, at least. I just hope it doesn't fade by the time it's my turn to perform.

I just wish I knew why this is so hard. But it's a question I know I can't answer, and instead of trying to figure it out, I turn my attention back to filling the straw dispensers.

As the night progresses, I realize one thing: Natalie'd definitely been right when she said that hardly anyone would be here to see me play. I'm pretty sure there are never more than five or six people in the cafe at the same time at all tonight, and most of them have only come to see a specific group play, and then left with them when their set ended. Not much of an open mic night, really, but that's okay with me.

It might actually be the perfect place for me to start, you know, playing for real.

I've got my head underneath the counter, scrubbing hard at some unidentifiable stain that's probably been here since before I was born, trying to keep my mind off what's about to happen, when the music stops and the last band before me finishes for the night. I'd told Natalie last week that I wanted to perform at the end -- I'd been hoping that the cafe would totally empty out by then.

"And now," Natalie says into the microphone so it echoes throughout the cafe, "I'd like to introduce Gemma's own Holly Shaw as she makes her musical debut!"

I stick my head out from under the counter and glance around; there are maybe three people in the entire place, plus Natalie and me. I can do this. I toss the rag aside and run into the back to grab my guitar and notebook.

And without really thinking about what's happening, I realize I'm suddenly sitting on the stool in the middle of the stage, my notebook open on the music stand in front of me. I strum a few chords on my guitar and even though my heart is beating wildly in my chest, I'm ready to begin singing when the bells jingle and the door to the cafe opens.

I squint past the bright lights to see who's walking in.

And when I do, I freeze, mouth open, hand hovering above the strings, eyes wide, breath caught in my throat.

Doan Riley and Justin have just come into Gemma's, and I feel a coldness sweep over me unlike anything I remember experiencing before.

It's over.

It never even began.

I can't play now.

Not with them here.

Why are they here?

I rest my guitar on the stage and hop off. Justin and Doan have slid onto stools at a high-top table in the corner and I stomp over to them in a huff of anger and disappointment.

"What are you doing here?" I demand, looking only at Doan.

"Hey, Holls, nice to see you, too," he says with an aggravating, cocky grin. I've seen it on him before, and I like it even less now. He doesn't look rattled at all. "Justin invited me."

I glare at him for a few seconds longer before swinging my attention over to my brother. "And who told you?"

"Uh, sorry, Holly. This is my fault."

I didn't hear Natalie creep up behind me, but she's standing there now, smiling apologetically at me, a sheepish half-smile on her face.

And suddenly I'm more confused than I am angry.

"You know my brother?" I ask.

Natalie nods. "Sure. We went to high school together."

"And you knew he was my brother?"

"We didn't figure it out until last weekend," Justin cuts in. "We kind of realized it by accident."

"Justin," I say through clenched teeth. "A word."

"Um," Natalie says. "Does this mean you're not going to play?"

I swing around to look at her. "Not tonight. Sorry. I'm sure the crowd is going to be disappointed." The last customer in the place -- a middle-aged man working on a laptop in the corner -- actually has earbuds in as he taps his converse sneakers to the beat of the music he's listening to.

Natalie nods once. "Okay. Don't worry about closing up. I was going to do it myself anyway."

"Great," I say, too flustered to realize that I don't want to leave her hanging. "Justin."

I stomp outside without looking at him and wait a few feet away from the entrance. A few seconds later, the bells above the door jingle as it's opened once more.

I have my back to him, but even though he doesn't say anything, I know he's there.

"You know I hate him," I snarl. "I can't believe you'd bring him with you to something like that."

There are a few beats of silence.

"Maybe he was interested in seeing more of what you're all about."

For the second time in as many minutes, I freeze. I may not have been back in Arizona all that long, but I still know the sound of my brother's voice, and that isn't it.

Slowly, I spin around.

Doan Riley is standing there, staring at me, no cockiness, no arrogance, no amusement etched anywhere on his face. Even his eyes aren't twinkling that annoying sparkle I'm so used to seeing in them.

"I said I wanted to talk to Justin."

"He was busy trying to tell Natalie that she didn't do a terrible thing by letting him know about you coming here tonight to sing," Doan says, lifting an eyebrow. "She feels really bad about that."

I shake my head, already feeling some of the tension seep out of my body. It isn't Natalie's fault that Doan is here right now. She didn't know I wouldn't want anyone to show up to see me for the first time, and you know what? I don't even think I'd have been all that mad if only Justin came. Maybe just -- I don't know -- surprised or something. But for him to bring Doan? Doan Riley? After everything? After we *talked* about this?

Yeah, I'm definitely not okay with it.

And Doan just so happens to be right in my line of fire.

"What are you *doing* here?" I demand.

"Justin invited me," he says again.

"That's great," I shoot back. "Maybe tomorrow he'll invite me to jump out of an airplane over Mount Everest without a parachute. Doesn't mean I'm going to say yes, you know."

Doan just shrugs. "But I wanted to."

"Yeah, clearly. Why?"

"I didn't have anything else going on tonight."

"You know I don't want you around me."

"You know you're not in charge of everything, right? I can show up wherever I want to."

I roll my eyes. "I didn't think you were the clingy type."

He flinches ever so slightly and I try to hold back my smile. Round One to Holly.

"Just the type with nothing better to do is all," he says. "Better than sitting around alone at home."

I'm not sure I believe him, but I don't tell him that. "Whatever, Doan. Why not just go race through the streets of Scottsdale some more? I bet there are lots of people out there who can't wait to run into you."

"Dammit, Holly! Will you let that go already?"

This explosion is more than I'm expecting and I take an involuntary step away.

"I already told you I won't do that."

Doan runs his hand over his mouth and sighs. "You really don't want me around?" There's no anger in his voice and his eyes only look tired.

"Everyone keeps saying you have all these reasons for why you act the way you do, but no one will tell me what they are. If I don't understand it, I can't get over it. It was just so stupid."

He drops down into one of the chairs at a table in front of the cafe and rests his elbows on his knees.

"They're right," he says, looking me straight in the eyes. I fold my arms across my chest. "I have reasons, and I have stories. Everybody has a story. But, Holly, what you have to understand is that not all of our stories are meant to be told. Mine are like that."

I stare down at the sidewalk. "No, I don't buy it," I say. "Because sometimes even if we don't want to share a story, it doesn't mean that we shouldn't. Sometimes, that's the best thing for us."

Doan looks up at me, nothing but sadness on his face, and I'm surprised. "Not this time," he says, his voice quiet. "You're just gonna have to trust me on that one."

Just a couple of minutes ago, I would have laughed in his face at this, but now all I do is drop down into the seat next to his and say nothing.

"I know that's a crazy thing for me to say to you," he goes on. "And there's no reason why you should. I get why you think I'm an asshole and you're not wrong because I think I'm an asshole, too. But I'm not all bad. I wasn't always all bad, anyway. I probably don't have any right to say this to you but I want to get to know you, Holly. You're not exactly making that easy for me, but I understand why. Just kind of hope maybe now you can give me a shot."

I raise my eyebrows. "A shot? At what?"

"Being your friend?" he says with a shrug of his shoulders. "I don't know. Not even that. Just maybe you don't have to hate seeing me all the time. We could start with that."

My eyes haven't left his face as he speaks, and I think back to what Justin told me, about how Doan wasn't always a bad guy and that the guy he once was is still somewhere inside him.

I think maybe I can sort of see that now.

I don't know, really. But it's not so crazy anymore.

Part of me -- more than the part that can't stand him -- wants to find out.

"I guess we'll see," I say at last.

He cracks a smile -- a real smile, not the cocky, arrogant grin I'm so used to seeing. "Good choice, Holls," he says. "You won't regret this."

He gets to his feet and walks away before I can say anything else.

And when I finally snap back to reality, I realize that I haven't even told him not to call me Holls.

CHAPTER ELEVEN

The next afternoon brings about my very first practice as a member of the Phoenix Scorpions. Justin had given me a T-shirt last night to wear to practice today, and as I slipped it on over my head and glanced in the mirror while getting dressed an hour earlier, I'd realized that I don't hate the way it looks on me.

It may not look right, but it isn't wrong, either.

It's clear now that maybe baseball isn't such a bad fit for me anymore.

And that isn't something I expected to find when I moved back here.

There's a pit in my stomach when Justin brings his BMW to a stop in the field's parking lot. I don't know if it's because I'm about to play baseball again or because I'm going to see Doan for the first time since open mic night at Gemma's, but I suddenly feel like I'm going to throw up all over the passenger seat of his car.

"You look pale," Justin says as we climb out and I reach into the backseat for the glove he let me borrow.

I glance down at myself. "You're just noticing this? You know I can't tan."

"No, I mean, you don't look good," he says, and I raise my eyebrows.

He sighs and kicks at the dirt. "You know what I mean."

I grin. "Yeah, but if this is how you talk to women, no wonder you're single."

"Is that what my problem is?"

I grab my gym bag out of the backseat and smile at him. "That's a longer conversation than what we've got time for right now."

Justin laughs, and I can't help but feel the uneasiness wash away. It's been so long since I've been able to relax and joke around with my brother; I missed it, a lot more than I thought I had.

My eyes scan the parking lot as Justin and I make our way over to the small cluster of guys gathered near the dugout. I don't see Doan's black pick-up truck yet, and part of me is relieved. I still don't know how I'm going to handle that situation.

Because I guess now I've agreed to be nice to him, and being nice to Doan Riley isn't going to be easy.

"Hey, Holly," Dad says, walking over to me and interrupting the conversation. "I have an idea. I'm sure you're pretty rusty on hitting so I thought I'd send you and one of our pitches out to the batting cages this afternoon so you can spend some time on your swing. Sound good?"

I frown. "I can't do that here?"

"You could," Dad says. "But I always like the cages, and I always send my guys out there when they're struggling at the plate."

"I'm not struggling at the plate."

He raises an eyebrow. "No, but you're not new to the game, either. You know what it's like when you don't have a groove."

I let out a sigh. "Sure, okay," I say. "I'll go."

Dad grins. "Great! Hey, Riley! Can you come over here for a second?"

I freeze and suddenly find myself hoping that there's a guy on the team whose first name is Riley.

But when Doan trots over to Dad and me with a huge grin on his face, I swallow hard.

I don't like where this is going.

I hadn't even realized he was here yet!

"You and Holly are going to spend the day at the cages," Dad says. "I want her to get used to swinging the bat again. It's been awhile since she's played. You good with that?"

"Whatever you say, Coach." He turns to me and smiles. "I hope you're ready for this, Holls."

I suck in a deep breath.

I'm pretty sure I'll never be quite ready for Doan Riley.

***

Doan opens the passenger side door to his pick-up truck and offers me a hand. I glance down at his outstretched palm, then hoist myself into the cab of the truck without his help. I look at him as he stares back at me, a crease in his forehead, before he closes the door and walks around to the driver's side.

I'm not sure what came over me, why I don't let him help me get up. It's a nice gesture -- maybe sweet, even -- and definitely unexpected coming from Doan, but I can't bring myself to put my hand in his.

I'm nervous, my palms sweating, as he buckles his seatbelt and revs the engine. I'm instantly brought back to the first time I ever saw him, his black pick-up truck screaming down Scottsdale Road and careening to a stop in a cloud of smoke, no care for anyone around him.

I have to imagine that he's thinking about the same thing I am. It's a quiet, awkward car ride to the batting cages. Despite how important baseball had been to me for so much of my life, I've never been to one before and I have no idea what to expect, or what it'll be like.

And the fact that Doan's going to be the one who teaches me doesn't really do a lot to put me at ease.

"This is my favorite place in Phoenix," he says as he guides his truck into the parking lot of a driving range.

"I don't need to work on my golf game," I reply. He parks the truck and cuts the engine; I let out a sigh. He turns sharply and looks at me.

"What was that?" he asks.

I glance over at him and raise an eyebrow. "What was what?"

"That sigh," he says, eyes boring into me. "You didn't trust me to drive here, did you?"

"I got into the car, didn't I?"

He rubs his forehead between his thumb and his index finger. "Let's just go hit."

I jump down from the truck, grab my bag and walk around to the driver's side. He's still sitting in his seat, and with the tinted windows, I can't see what he's doing inside. I'm about to turn and walk in without him when the car door opens and he hops out, baseball bag slung over his shoulder.

He tucks a pack of cigarettes into the pocket of his shorts, and I'm surprised to see it, but don't say anything.

I've never been to this place before but it's clear from the whirring red lights and buzzing chimes and clangs of the carnival games that there's way more to it than just being a simple driving range. Picture any game you can imagine; I'm sure you'll find it here. Screaming children run in every direction and the sickening sugary smell of cotton candy turns my stomach.

I'm not sure if it's from the sweetness of the food or the nerves I seem to get whenever I'm around Doan.

But I feel my head start to pound almost instantly. Doan leads me through the maze of games and kids, and out back to a patio where we get in line to buy tickets for mini golf, bumper boats, sand volleyball courts and the batting cages.

"Oh, mini golf," I say without even really thinking about it. I turn to see if I can spot the courses. "I love it so much. I haven't played in such a long time."

He looks over at me. "Really? I do it all the time on weekends."

I don't know why, but this surprises me. Doan doesn't really strike me as the type to spend a Saturday night on the putt-putt course.

I'm about to say something else when the customer in front of us steps aside and Doan walks up to the window, pays for the cages and hands me a helmet.

"I have money," I say, reaching into my bag for my wallet.

"Don't be dumb," he replies, holding the helmet out to me.

"Seriously?" I ask, looking at it in his hand.

He nods. "Same thing as in a game. Those balls are still coming at you fast, you know."

I sigh; I'd never balk at wearing a batting helmet in a real game, but I feel incredibly dorky putting it on over my hair now.

Doan tucks his own helmet in the crook of his elbow and I follow him over to the batting cages.

"Start with this one," he says. "The pitches will come at you at 80 miles per hour." We walk inside a chain-link enclosure and he shows me where to stand on the home plate.

Doan feeds a machine several tokens, then takes a step back.

"Are you ready?" he asks, shooting me a small, unexpected smile.

I take a deep breath. "Ready as I'll ever be."

Doan gives me a funny look, but I'm barely paying attention to him right now. My knees are bent, arms about shoulder-high, bat raised above my head, eyes trained on the machine that's about to send balls flying at me from across the park.

The rotating arm winds up and fires the first yellow ball at me. I keep my eyes focused on it as it flies toward me. I bring my arms around and swing as hard as I can.

The ball hits the vinyl screen hanging on the fence behind me with a thud and I realize that I completely whiffed on the pitch.

I can't stop a small, frustrated sigh from squeaking out between my lips. I don't know what happened to me; I used to be money with a baseball bat in my hands. Now I can't even make enough contact with the ball to foul it off.

"It's okay, Holly," Doan says from my left. "Just get ready for the next one."

I square up to the machine a second time and wait for the pitch. It flies toward me and I close my eyes and hack at it.

I'm not surprised when it slams into the vinyl behind me.

Doan's chuckling softly when I open my eyes.

"That's a different strategy," he says, and I look at him sharply but there's no malice in his eyes, just a friendly, easygoing twinkle I'm not sure I ever remember seeing from him before. "But maybe we should try one that's a little bit more, uh, effective."

I laugh despite my frustrations. "I don't know what's wrong here."

He walks over to the token machine and hits the red pause button. "Okay," he says. "I know you didn't really ask for my help but I'm here and I think I have a few ideas."

I shrug. "It's not like I can get any worse."

He nods, and I think about being offended that he's agreeing that I suck but decide it isn't worth it.

Besides, he's not wrong.

He comes up and stands just slightly behind me, close enough that I think I can feel his breath on the back of my neck, but I'm also not sure if that's just the warm desert breeze.

"Right now, your batting stance is pretty typical," he says, and I look at him over my shoulder as he mirrors my pose. "Let's change that up and see how it works. So line up as you were on home plate. We're gonna close off your stance for more power."

He waits as I get myself into the position I'm so used to assuming whenever I'm about to hit a baseball -- even if it's been years since it's happened. For me, I guess, playing baseball is like riding a bicycle; it's something I'll never forget how to do, even if I'm not good at it anymore.

"See how you have your feet squared up to the plate?" he asks, and I look down, then nod. "Try taking your foot that's closest to the pitcher's mound and place it a little bit closer to home."

I do as he suggests and I'm surprised when he bursts out laughing. "Not like that," he says. "Too much. Move it back a little."

I glare at him slightly as he directs my movements until I'm settled into a stance that he thinks looks good.

"And that's it?" I ask as he takes a step back toward the machine to resume the pitches.

He nods. "We'll see if it works. I have a few other ideas, too, though," he says, then presses the green start button.

I take a deep breath and wait the pitch. As it flies toward me, I swing and make contact, but the ball sails straight up in the air and bounces off the vinyl behind me.

"That's okay," Doan says, clapping his hands together. "At least you hit it."

He's right. It's more than I've been able to do since I picked up my bat again.

The next pitch comes at me; I wiggle the bat above my head, eye trained on the ball and at just the last second, I swing through the pitch, putting all of the power from my legs into the hit.

And sure enough, the ball flies out toward the machine and clangs into the chain-link fence on the other side.

"Well, I don't know about you," Doan says, "but I'm pretty sure if that fence wasn't there, you'd have just hit a home run."

It didn't feel like a home run swing to me, but I smile at him anyway, and he returns my grin.

For the first time since I've known him, I don't really want to fight with Doan.

***

"I think I'm done," I say after my fifth hit in a row. I've settled into a groove and I'm feeling pretty good about baseball right now.

"You sure?" Doan asks.

"Oh yeah. This is going too well. I don't want to ruin the vibe if I start going cold again."

He smiles at me. "I get that," he says. "But I think you're good with this new stance. Let's bring the helmets back if you're done."

I pull the batting helmet off of my sweaty hair and fluff it out with my fingers as Doan and I walk side-by-side back up to the ticket office.

"Can I get two for mini golf?" Doan asks the booth attendant, digging his wallet out of the back pocket of his pants.

"Wait, what?" I turn to him with a frown on my face.

He looks down at me and grins. "You said you love it but you haven't played in awhile. We're here so why not go for it, right?"

I look at him, surprised he even remembers I made a comment about playing mini golf at all. It just doesn't seem like something someone like him would pick up on.

"Well, okay." I smile at him. "Let's do it."

He shakes his head like he isn't sure what to think before he passes the attendant a twenty. She hands him his change, then pushes two putters across the counter toward us, and Doan holds them out to me.

"Pick a color, any color," he says.

She's given us a pink club and a green club, and I reach for the green one, then grab a purple ball to go with it.

"Well," Doan says, looking down at the club I left him with. "I'm all about matching my shoes to my purse, so I think I better go with the pink ball, too."

I can't hide my smile. "The color suits you."

"So you any good at this?" he asks as he tucks a scorecard into the back pocket of his shorts and we walk out toward the courses.

"Mini golf? Hell yeah. I'm a pro."

"Good," he says. "Then you don't care if we play the hard course, right?"

"Bring it."

He laughs. "Oh, it's on now."

I walk right up to the first tee and drop my purple ball onto the green. There are painted numbers on the sidewalk in front of the hole that indicate this round is a par 3. I vow to knock it in with just two strokes.

Suddenly, all I can do is think about beating Doan Riley.

I line my club up with the ball and carefully study the layout of the hole in front of me.

"Serious business," Doan jokes from behind me.

I spin around to look at him. "Hey now," I say with mock indignation. "I have a process here. You might be an asshole but I don't think you're the type of guy who wants to be known as a cheater at mini golf, too."

He flashes me an angelic, innocent smile. "Ah, you don't know me at all, Holls," he says. "But by all means, if you need perfect conditions to play your game, who am I to get in the way of that? I want to beat you at your best."

I shake my head and smirk, then go back to concentrating on the ball. One practice putt later and I hit the ball, angling it to swing around the curve in the course and hopefully dump right into the cup at the other end for a hole in one.

The ball hits the bump in the green just as I want it to but it rolls to the left of the cup and comes harmlessly to a stop near the hole; it's an easy putt but not my best play. I narrow my eyes.

"Not bad, not bad," Doan says, stepping up to the tee and dropping his pink ball onto the green. He hits it a second later, not bothering to line it up with the curve, and it predictably comes to a stop several feet away from the hole.

Good.

He frowns slightly.

"What's the matter?" I ask him. "Didn't go as planned?"

He shoots me a look. "You ever hear of just playing for fun?"

I pretend to think about this for a few seconds.

"Nope," I reply. "I don't know what that means."

He shakes his head. "Figures."

I don't know if I like the way he says this, like we're suddenly not just teasing each other anymore.

"Something wrong?"

"Not at all." He nods in the direction of my ball. "Go make your putt."

I frown but I do like he says and tap the purple ball into the hole. "That's two for me," I say.

Doan doesn't acknowledge my comment as he hits his ball toward the hole, but it goes well right of the cup and he lets out a frustrated sigh, and I can't keep the scowl off my face. I'm not sure what happened to upset him so much but I do know that I don't like it.

And that's almost as weird to me as his shift in attitude is.

He tosses his ball down onto the green and whacks at it. I'm not surprised when it doesn't end up anywhere near the hole.

I carefully place mine down and hit it with just as much precision as last time. It rolls around the lip of the cup once, then drops in for a hole-in-one. I smile and look at him, but he isn't meeting my eye.

"Okay," I say at last, any teasing gone from my voice. "What's your deal?"

"Nothing. Let's just play."

I roll my eyes. "Obviously it isn't nothing."

He sighs. "No one ever taught you how to be a gracious winner, huh?"

I snap my head up. "What?"

"Nothing. I just don't like sore winners."

"Uh, well, good," I say with a shrug. "Because I don't see any of those here."

He raises his eyebrows. "Oh, really?"

"Doan, what are you talking about? Sorry that I'm playing competitively, but that's just who I am."

"It isn't that," he says. "But the whole gloating thing when I botched the first shot? Come on, Holly."

"Are you kidding?"

There's a funny faraway look on his face -- one that I've never seen him wear before -- like he's standing here with me but he isn't really *with me*, if you know what I mean.

Doan shakes his head quickly. "Sorry," he says, furrowing his brow. "Sorry. I just -- you reminded me a lot of my brother then. Sorry."

"The solider?" I ask.

He nods.

"You miss him?"

Doan gives me a funny look. "Yeah," he says, his voice quiet but clear and unlike anything I've heard from him yet. "Yeah. Everyday."

"I guess you guys're close then."

Doan walks over and finishes out the hole before he goes on to the next one. I follow him in silence.

"You could say that," he finally says.

I line up my shot and send it in toward the hole, but I'm suddenly less focused on the game. There's something about the way Doan's talking now, the way he's carrying himself. I want to give him all of my attention.

What he's saying somehow just seems...important. Like I need to hear this. I don't know what it is.

"How long has it been?" I ask, my voice quiet.

"About six months."

"That's not that bad," I say.

He gives me a funny look. "I don't know," he says. "I think any time at all is too much."

I'm surprised by the bite in his voice.

"Yeah, of course," I say quickly. "Sorry. I guess it's different for me and Justin."

"Yeah. I'd say so."

Doan whacks his ball toward the sixth hole and finishes it out in two strokes. I line up for my turn.

"I hadn't seen my brother in five years," I tell him. "Until I came back here last week. And even then, the one time I did see him was just to go to my dad's wedding. We haven't spent more than a week together in the last decade."

"Like you didn't even have a brother at all," he says.

I nod. "Exactly. And Justin and I were close before my mom and I moved. I mean, we all were. Baseball kept us together until it was what tore us apart."

I'm surprised to find tears prickling at the corners of my eyes as I hit the ball, but I'm hardly paying attention to golf right now. I haven't bothered to line up my shot and the ball goes shooting into the brick wall lining the course and bounces into a mini sand trap.

But I couldn't care less about that right now.

Doan's eyes are boring into me, and I feel the heat seeping into my skin underneath the intensity of his gaze.

"How?" he asks.

I shake my head. "It's so cliche. Happens to so many kids."

He stares at me. "Maybe, but it still happened to you, right?"

"Yeah."

"Then how?"

"My dad was sent from Arizona to Colorado at the trade deadline," I say in a rush. It's a story I don't usually tell, and if I'm going to talk about it, I want it to be over quickly. "He said he'd go for a couple of months, then come back when the season ended. He did all of that."

I hit my ball toward the cup at the next hole and sigh. Doan waits quietly for me to continue.

"Thing is, he came back with someone else," I say, keeping my eyes trained down on the green. "He didn't come back for us. Or all of us, anyway." I shake my head and brush at the tears clinging to the inner corners of my eyes. "Sorry. I don't know why I'm telling you all of this. You don't care."

Doan rolls his eyes. "I asked, didn't I? I think it's pretty obvious at this point that I care."

"Why?"

He shrugs. "I told you from the beginning, I just like getting to know other people's stories."

"But you won't share yours."

He shakes his head. "No."

I offer him a small smile. "Maybe we'll talk about this some other time."

"You can tell me, Holly."

I search his face, and it's friendly and warm, and I believe him that he'll listen and maybe even understand, and it'd probably be good to talk about all of this after so long.

But I don't think I'm ready.

"I know I can," I tell him, and I mean it. "But not today."

I realize we've been standing at the start of the next hole without either of us making a move to play it. Doan must have come to the same conclusion because he reaches over and gently takes the club and ball out of my hands, and silently leads me off the course.

We walk over to a small pond with a fountain in the middle. Doan drops onto the grassy slope next to the water, and I sit down next to him.

Neither of us says anything for a few beats.

"You know," I say after a minute. "It's weird being here like this. With you."

He looks over at me with a small smile. "Why's that?"

"I couldn't stand you from the moment I met you."

He lets out a long laugh. "You don't waste words, do you?"

"Never have."

I lay down on the grass so I'm staring up at the clear night sky. He leans back so he's propping himself up on his elbow and looks over at me.

"What's your family like?" I ask him.

He looks over at me, eyebrows raised. "What?"

"We've spent all this time talking about why I should spend more time with mine. Maybe I want to know more about yours."

Doan shakes his head. "Holly."

"Seriously?" I throw up my hands. "This is off-limits, too? Come on. You asked me to be friends and I'm trying here but if you can't give me an answer even one time when I have a question, this is pointless."

"He studies me for a long moment, then digs into his pants pocket and pulls out a pack of cigarettes and a red lighter. I watch as he carefully pries open the container and slides one cigarette out.

I wrinkle my nose but don't say anything. It's his turn to talk.

"You're asking a lot, you know that, right?" He brings the cigarette to his lips.

"I don't think I am. And if anything, this is really your fault."

He breathes in, looks over at me and smiles. "Oh, is that so?"

I nod. "You keep talking about how important family is. It's not my fault I want to know more about yours now."

"You're a real pain in the butt sometimes, you know that, Holls?" he says, then he sighs. "I had a really normal family growing up. Mom, Dad, two brothers. I'm the middle kid."

He stops, looks at me and waits as if he expects me to make some kind of snarky remark here, but I don't want to interrupt.

"We did normal family stuff," he goes on. "Still do. Vacations and holidays and sports." He shrugs. "But my brother's deployment kind of changed all that. Especially in my mom."

I nod. "I can imagine," I say quietly.

"Yeah. We didn't even have Christmas the first year he was gone," he says. "He couldn't celebrate with a tree and stockings and fire and hot chocolate, well, neither would we."

Doan takes a deep breath and I can see he's starting to get uncomfortable.

"It's been hard," he says. "Getting used to all of it. It's like waking up from a really vivid dream. You're in the middle of this crazy life and it feels so real and then you open your eyes and that's gone and you're somewhere else entirely. Sometimes even someone else, you know? That's what it's been like."

I think about my mom meeting the count and my move out here, and I nod and before I even realize what I'm doing, I'm reaching out and gently stroking his shoulder.

I don't mean it as anything more than support, but he puts his hand over mine and squeezes once before letting go.

"And it's hard because I don't want to make it worse for my parents but it's like they're expecting so much more from me and I can't always come through," he blurts out, and I suck in a breath, sure there's a deeper story behind these words.

"Don't I know how that goes," I mutter.

He looks over at me. "Oh, yeah? How?"

I wave a hand dismissively. "The whole college thing. My parents are still horrified that I'm not sure I want to go in the fall."

"Why don't you?"

"I don't know. Not sure it's right. We talked about this."

"I know," he says. "But if this isn't right, then what is?"

"I don't know that, either," I tell him, and he smiles.

"Maybe that's the problem. I bet your parents would be way better with this if you actually had a plan or something."

"Maybe. Or maybe it's just because I'm not doing what they think I should be. It wouldn't be the first time."

"I guess I don't know about that," he concedes. "But my advice, even if it means nothing to you?"

I nod.

"Go to college," he says. "You told me you got into ASU. Go for a semester. There's only one way to know if something's really right for you. You've gotta try it."

I don't say anything.

"Besides," he tells me. "If you don't do something, you can only miss out. If you try it and hate it, well, at least you know, right? That's gotta be better than sitting around and wondering."

"That...actually makes sense," I tell him, and he laughs.

"Don't sound so surprised. I'm not an idiot all the time."

"Only when you drive, right?" I tease.

He holds up the pack of cigarettes in his hand. "And smoke. But that's a different story."

I let that comment go and Doan gets to his feet and holds out his hand to me, and this time I put mine in his and he helps me up.

"It's late," he says. "I should get you home."

I search his face for a few seconds, surprised to realize I'm disappointed the night's coming to an end.

"Yeah," I say, dropping his hand. "You're probably right."

CHAPTER TWELVE

I'm not excited to suit up for my first baseball game as a member of Dad's team, but there isn't much I can do about that as Saturday afternoon rolls around and we're just half an hour away from the opening pitch of the summer season.

I haven't seen Doan since the night at the batting cages, and I'm not sure what to think about that.

He hadn't seemed particularly bothered by the depth our conversation, but it's been eating at me since it happened. I can't get it out of my head, and I definitely can't figure out how to align that Doan with the Doan I thought I knew since I got here.

His sweetness and his sincerity after mini golf are nothing like the guy I remember from my first day in town.

And definitely nothing like the guy I saw in the hallway the other day coming out of the bathroom. I can't get that out of my head, either -- the look on his face as he scanned me from head to toe in my towel, the glimmer of heat in his golden brown eyes, the cocky tone of his voice.

That's all classic Doan Riley, exactly what I've come to expect from him since I first met him.

But it isn't that simple this time, because now I know him better.

And I guess maybe it's about learning to take the bad with the good and all that nonsense. No one likes everything about anyone. It's just deciding whether you're willing to put up with all the crap because the good stuff makes you happy enough to get through anything else.

Maybe I'm just not sure it does yet with Doan.

Justin's words keep rattling around in my head and mixing with what I felt sitting next to Doan after mini golf the other night.

My brother called me blind, said I can't see Doan. I'm not sure what, exactly, he means by that, but I can't get it off my mind, and I don't know why. It shouldn't matter to me this much.

And the worst part about it?

I'm not mad about Doan's comments in the hallway yesterday, not even a little bit. The blush in my cheeks pretty much gives it away that there's something about Doan, something I don't quite understand.

Maybe it's more that I'm mad at myself for not being able to figure out what's going on here. I'm not used to this, being so rattled around someone all the time. And I'm definitely not used to having to revise my first impression of people. Doan, I'd been convinced, was a jerk, an asshole of the highest order, and now I have no idea what to make of him.

And *that* is something I know I don't like.

I bring my car to a stop in the parking lot and hop out, already dressed in my uniform for the game. I'm late, no surprise, and it looks like everyone else is already here, gathered on the field warming up.

I grab my baseball bag and make my way over to the dugout, where Dad's standing alone.

"Holly!" The relief on his face is almost palpable when he catches sight of me. "You made it!"

I give him a funny look. "Of course I did."

"I, uh -- I wasn't sure you were going to show up," he says, his cheeks coloring.

"I gave you my word I'd play, right?"

He nods, looking much more comfortable and relaxed. "Go get out on the field with the rest of the team."

I leave my bag in the dugout after pulling out my glove, and I trot onto the outfield grass.

Doan and my brother are throwing a ball back and forth when I approach, and both stop and look at me.

"Heads up," Justin says, tossing the ball my way.

I reach up with my glove and snag it out of the air, then toss it to Doan without really glancing his way.

"Nice throw, Holls," he says as the ball lands in the leather mitt of his glove. "Remember your stance today, right?"

I force myself to look at him and he's smiling kindly back at me, a tentative, unsure smile that I try to tell myself I don't find endearing at all.

But I do.

Dammit.

I nod at him. "I got it down. I even practiced it last night."

He grins. "Really?"

"Yep. In front of the mirror. Better work or I'm gonna be looking for a new coach," I say, hoping to ease some of the awkwardness that I feel by making a joke.

It seems to work because Doan's shoulders relax as he tosses the ball to Justin, who slings it at me. The three of us laugh as we discuss the upcoming season opener against a similar collegiate league team from northern Arizona.

It's all normal and great and going fine until Dad blows his whistle and it's time for the game to start. My stomach twists, and I'm suddenly afraid I'm going to throw up.

It's time to return to baseball.

The lineup card hanging in the dugout has me batting sixth, right after Justin and just before Doan, who's on the pitcher's mound tonight.

We take the field as the visiting team -- the Flagstaff Flyers -- is up to bat first.

I'm playing third base, as I've always done since I was a kid. It's strange to take my place on the diamond; it's been so long since it's happened for real that I'm afraid it's not going to feel right, and while it doesn't exactly seem completely natural right now, it isn't wrong, either.

I'm okay with it.

And I know it'll work out.

I watch Doan toss his warm-up pitches to the catcher, taking in everything from the way he bites his lower lip just before each throw to the flex of his thighs as he releases the ball, and I try to tear my eyes off of him, but it's not working so great.

This, I know, is a dangerous, dangerous path I'm starting to wander down. I don't trust Doan. I'm not sure what happened to harden him, but I can't just ignore that there's something about him -- something crucial -- that I don't know. I can't ignore how I met him, how angry he made me, how stupid he was, how arrogant and cocky he acted toward me.

And, despite all of that, I also can't ignore how he made my stomach flip and palms sweat when he rolled down the tinted window of his pick-up truck and I saw him for the first time. I can't ignore how he made me feel talking to him during mini golf the other night.

And I definitely can't ignore the way I can't help but bite my lip and stare every time I see him without his shirt on.

Dangerous.

I snap out of my trance as the game begins. The first batter for the Flyers steps up to the plate and Doan stares in as the catcher signals the pitch. I force myself to pay attention to the game and not just watch him.

Doan deals the pitch, high and wide, and the batter lets it sail past him for ball one. The batter resets, Doan and the catcher agree on what to throw, and he tries again.

This time, the batter swings at it and sends it flying toward the shortstop. I panic momentarily, forgetting what I'm supposed to do in this situation. Is it my ball to play? No, no. John's got it. Relax, Holly.

John scoops up the bouncing ball and fires it to the first basemen, who easily steps on the bag ahead of the runner and makes the first out of the game. I let out a sigh of relief, glad I hadn't had to do anything to make the play.

The second batter pops out to center field, and the third strikes out.

I breathe in and out as I jog back to the dugout to watch our first three hitters take a stab at the Flyers pitcher.

I don't like how unsettled I felt out there. It seems so abnormal right now, being back on the field like this. I'm struggling with returning to the game, maybe more than I thought I would.

I'm not up to bat right away so I watch as our first three hitters go down in order.

And just like that, it's time for me to go back out onto the field, and I can't ignore the growing pit in my stomach.

Something's definitely off here.

It doesn't get any better even when the ball bounces my way and I make an easy throw to first base for the final out of the inning.

Doan wanders over to me in the dugout. "Everything going okay out there?" he asks.

I smile tightly and nod, trying to paint a calm look on my face. "It's dandy," I say, then immediately cringe.

To his credit, Doan looks at me skeptically. "Dandy, huh?" he says. "You sure you want to stick with that story?"

I can't help but let out a small, nervous chuckle. "It's not that easy going back out there."

He nods. "I get it. You'll settle in, though. I was the same way when I first started playing in Tucson."

"Yeah? Even in college?"

"Oh, definitely in college," he says. "That was the worst of it. It really counts, then, you know? Pressure's on. But here? Relax. Have fun with it. That's all it's about."

I smile at him, and I mean it this time. "Thanks," I say. "Really. That helps."

He grins and winks at me before tapping the brim of my baseball hat. "Anytime," he says, then walks away to talk to my brother.

I smile and drop down onto the bench, feeling better now than I have all day.

My positive mood is all but gone after the game.

Let's just say, it ended right after my final appearance at the plate, and let's also just say, it ended with the umpire yelling 'Steeeee-rike three!' right in my ear.

Because let me tell you, it's every girl's dream to lose a baseball game for her team by striking out looking.

But no one seems particularly bothered by it in the dugout except for me. Most of the guys are talking, laughing, whistling. Dad and Justin are grinning in the corner, but I'm just sitting on the bench, kicking at the floor with the toe of my shoe.

"Quit pouting." Doan drops down onto the seat next to me. "It's one game."

"I'm not pouting," I say, folding my arms across my chest, and he laughs.

"Oh, no?" he says. "That's not what this is?"

I shake my head and puff out my bottom lip for dramatic effect. "I'd never do that."

"'Course not," he says. "Come on, let's go grab some ice cream."

"Ice cream?" I repeat.

"Yeah." He hesitates. "Unless you don't want to be seen in public with me. I totally understand."

I laugh and swat at his arm. "Oh, stop. I think I can handle it."

He smiles at me, and it's a genuine smile that sends a ripple straight down to my belly.

"There's a place on Indian Bend and 55th," he tells me. "I'll meet you there."

I hop into my Honda and pull out of the parking lot before he does. I don't want it to seem like I'm following his car or anything.

The ice cream parlor is just a few minutes away and he pulls in right behind me.

"After you," he says, holding open the door to the building for me, and I step inside.

"What can I get you?" the girl behind the counter asks immediately. I look over at Doan but he's still deciding and indicates that I should go ahead and order.

"Can I just get a small cup of soft vanilla with rainbow sprinkles, please?" I ask.

The girl nods, and I turn around to find Doan staring at me.

"What?" I say.

"That's it? Vanilla ice cream and rainbow sprinkles?"

I nod. "That's what I like."

"Even when you could have peanut butter cup and fudge and caramel and that hard chocolate stuff that freezes on top?"

"Even then," I tell him, and he shakes his head but smiles.

"You're a strange one, you know that?" he says.

"Never claimed otherwise," I tell him as I take the cup from the girl.

Doan orders a double scoop of banana ice cream with caramel and walnuts and whipped cream. I move down to the cash register to pay for them when he immediately swats me away.

"Stop that," he says. "I got it."

I'm pleased he takes the bait. "If you insist. Thanks."

It's almost dark out now so the temperature's fallen to a comfortable 80 degrees with a nice, light breeze, and we decide to take our ice cream to a bench outside.

We eat in easy, comfortable silence until Doan turns to me.

"So," he says. "I know you like baseball and all. But what's up with this now? Why'd you agree to play for your dad? Thought you didn't want to do that."

I know he's thinking back to our conversation outside my bedroom last week when he warned me that Dad was going to invite me to play for the team.

I'd been so against it then, and now here I am.

It's a fair question, even if it does sort of feel like I never get to ask him any of my own.

"It's actually really simple," I say after thinking about it for a second. "I was going to say no. I had no intentions of playing again. But then he asked me and yes was the only word I could get out."

Doan smiles before looking down at his ice cream. "Really?"

I nod. "Yeah. Believe me, I didn't expect that."

"Me, neither," he replies. "Not after the look on your face when I told you what I'd heard."

"Like I said, it was just really not something I was thinking about. It caught me off guard."

"Are you glad you're doing it?"

I smile. "So far. I wish today would've gone better, though."

He waves his spoon in the air. "Can't worry about that. If I wrote down a list of all the games I want back in my career, we'd sit out here until next season."

"I guess."

"Trust me on that." He looks over at me and sees the empty ice cream cup in my hand. "Done with that?"

I hand it to him. "Thanks," I say as he walks a few feet away to the trash can. He comes back, stops in front of me and digs something out of the pocket of his jeans.

A pack of cigarettes.

He lights one, brings it to his lips and inhales. Then he looks at me.

"What?" Doan asks. "Not going to say anything about this?"

"About what?" I reply, raising my eyebrows.

He looks surprised. "I'm used to the lectures when someone finds out I'm a smoker."

I shrug. "Your choice. It's not like I'm going to come up with some new info you don't have about why it's stupid."

He looks at me and laughs. "That's why I like you," he says, and I swallow hard when I feel my heart start to beat a little faster. "You've got a way with words, Holls. I don't know what it is."

I shrug. "I like writing. I better be good at it."

"I don't know if that's it," he says. "But I like that I can look at you and know exactly what you're thinking."

I grimace, and he laughs, and I'm horrified.

I'm pretty sure Doan thinking he can read my mind or something is definitely not going to end well for me at all.

CHAPTER THIRTEEN

"What are you doing tonight?"

I'm perched on the bar stool in the kitchen early the next morning with a bowl of cereal and a mug of hot coffee when Justin pops in and wanders over to the fridge. His hair is still disheveled and he hasn't changed out of his pajamas.

I shrug. "Haven't thought about it."

"Seriously? Do you even know what day it is?" he asks. "How could you not have plans?"

"No," I say, thinking it over in my head. "What day is it?"

He turns around and stares at me. "It's the fourth of July, Holls." He pulls the orange juice out of the fridge and closes the door. "That settles it. You're coming out with us."

"Fourth of July?" I repeat. "I've been here for more than a month already?"

He looks at me and grins. "That so hard to believe? Not as bad as you thought it would be, right?"

I stare at him, mouth hanging open slightly. I had no idea it was already July 4th. I mean, sure, I know it's July and all, but it just never really felt like the holiday was approaching.

"I guess not." I return his smile. "What are you guys doing?"

"Doan's dad has a boat," Justin says. "We thought we'd take it out on the lake. We usually do it every year."

My stomach tightens at the sound of Doan's name.

"Oh," I say, trying to casually brush the sweat on my palms off on my shorts. "I think I'm good."

Justin just smiles at me. "Yeah, right. You're not sitting around at home with Dad and Tanya on the Fourth, Holls. I won't let you."

"Yeah, but I don't -- "

"No buts about it," he cuts in. "You have no good reason for not coming with us."

"Actually, I --"

"Nope. I don't care about whatever's going on with you and Doan. You're coming."

I feel my cheeks flush. "Nothing's going on with me and Doan," I protest.

"Good." Justin grins. "Then there's no reason you shouldn't want to come."

I let out a sigh. He's got me, and he knows it, and so do I.

"When do we leave?"

"Half an hour."

My eyes widen. "You think I can be ready that fast?"

Justin shrugs, a devilish gleam in his eye. "Remember you don't care about anyone that's going, right? You should be ready in five minutes."

I glare at him, don't say anything and hurry out of the room. I can hear him chuckling softly behind me as he puts the milk back in the fridge.

***

Justin stops his BMW in a sandy parking lot in front of a wide lake resting in the valley of several different mountains lining it on all sides. My jaw drops slightly at how beautiful the scene in front of me is; I've never seen anything like this.

The lake is huge, bigger than I remember it being the last time I came here when I was just a kid. Hundreds of tiny specks litter the water's surface -- islands. They're small, of course, even when you get close to them in a boat, but they're just big enough to pilot over to and lay out on.

And the way the sunlight reflects off the mountains, making them glow red even at mid-morning -- it's beautiful. Breathtaking, even.

Justin opens his car door and startles me out of my trance.

With one last longing look, I unbuckle my seatbelt and hop out of the car. I glance around subtly behind my sunglasses, looking for Doan.

I find him standing knee deep in the water, wiping at something on the side of the boat with a blue rag. I see him before he sees me, and I'm glad. It's like when you spot an enemy spider crawling across your bedroom ceiling late at night and you can't let it out of your sight because the very second you do, it disappears, and then you can't sleep, and it sneaks up and attacks when you least it expect it.

Yeah.

I'm not about to let Doan be that spider.

I stand here for a few seconds until Justin sneaks up behind me.

"Enjoying the view?" he asks, startling me from my thoughts.

I spin around, hand over my suddenly rapidly-beating heart. "Jesus, Justin, you scared me."

He grins devilishly at me. "You didn't answer my question."

I glare at him. "It's really pretty here," I say, raising my eyebrows as if I'm issuing some sort of challenge, and I think I might be.

But my brother only laughs. "Oh, Holls," he says. "And you think Doan's the crazy one."

I don't respond, and when I glance over to where I last saw Doan standing, I realize he's gone.

Just like the spider.

Great.

"Come on, give me a hand with this thing."

My brother points to the cooler he packed this morning before we left the house. I bend down to pick up one end and he grabs the other before walking backwards down toward the shoreline.

Meanwhile, I'm nervous the whole time because I can't keep an eye on Doan.

"Here's good," Justin says, and I release the end I'm holding. The cooler drops down onto the ground with a thud, kicking up a cloud of sand. He shoots me a dirty look because he hadn't let go of his side yet, but I barely notice.

My brother walks away to get more of the stuff he brought with us out of the car, and leaves me standing alone awkwardly near the boat. I look around, trying to find something to do so I don't look out of place, but there's nothing -- and no one -- I recognize.

"Let's get that on board."

I spin around, heart instantly in my throat. Sure enough, Doan's crept up behind me and I hadn't noticed him coming.

"What?" I say, stomach twisting just at the sight of him.

He lifts an eyebrow, then points down at the ground without taking his eyes off of me.

"The cooler," he says like my idiocy amuses him, and probably it does. "We want that on the boat. Help me bring it on."

"Fine," I snap, my tone harsh mostly because I'm embarrassed. "You don't have to talk to me like I'm five."

He shakes his head but says nothing, and we both lean down to grab an end. I look at the boat floating easily in shallow waters and don't see any kind of ramp or dock to get on.

"How are we going to get this on there?" I ask.

"Boy you're on a roll today," he says, and I suppress the urge to let go of the cooler and give him a kick where it'll hurt. "See the boat? See the really shallow water? You walk through it. And there's a ladder on the other side."

I glare at him. "How am I supposed to know that?"

He laughs. "Don't be so testy, Holls. I'm just messing with you."

"Yeah, well, maybe I don't want to be messed with," I mutter under my breath. He isn't supposed to hear me, but he lets out a low chuckle anyway.

"And that's what makes it so much fun for me."

I shake my head. Every time he does something to make me think maybe he isn't the total asshole I pegged him for on day one, he does something else to bring me right back to my initial conclusion about him.

And it bugs me that I still can't let it go, let him go, that I can't tell him to piss off and let me forget him. He does just enough to keep me dying to know his story. Walking away is the right thing, the smart thing, and yet it's the only thing I can't figure out how to do.

And it's making me kind of crazy.

I'm wearing flip-flops and a sundress so wading through the shallow, wonderfully cool waters is no big deal. Doan glances back at me after we take a few steps in as if he expects me to protest or complain, but the water feels nice and refreshing lapping at the skin around my ankles hot from the sun.

"What, not too cold for you?"

I shake my head. "It's perfect."

"Surprising."

"Why?"

"I thought girls like you always squeal when you get in the water," he replies. "'It's too cold! It's too cold! I can't get in there!'"

"Don't go into acting," I tell him as I try not to laugh at his terrible impression of a girl. "Your falsetto isn't exactly impressive."

He wiggles his eyebrows at me, and it's like all the tension he caused me just minutes ago disappears. He has an uncanny way of doing that to me. It's that damn hook again.

And that makes me kind of crazy, too.

"If that's the least impressive thing about me, then I think I'm doing okay," he says, and that shuts me up pretty fast. I have no idea how to respond.

He leads me through the rest of the water and right around to the back side of the boat that wasn't visible from the shore, and sure enough, there's a ladder going straight down into the water.

"Pass me the cooler and climb up," he says, and I do. When I'm securely on deck, I turn around to take the cooler from him.

He's reaching over to me with it and I grab for it, but it must've gotten wet or I don't get a good enough grip because it slips out of my hands and tumbles down into the water. It floats there for a second or two, then sinks, but the water's so shallow that the top of the cooler doesn't submerge all the way.

Doan and I stare at it for a few beats, then look at each other before bursting out laughing.

"I don't even know why this is funny," he says, and I try to nod in-between heaves of my shoulders. "It really isn't."

He's holding onto the railing of the ladder for support with one hand and pressing his fingers into the corner of his eyes with the other to keep the tears from leaking out. I'm just standing on deck, my shoulders shaking, no sound coming out of my mouth.

When Doan gets a hold of himself, he looks at me. "Is that really how you laugh?" he asks. "Or were you just faking it?"

I try to pull myself together. "No," I say. "Usually when things are super funny to me, I laugh so hard that I don't make any noise. Like that."

He stares at me, the teasing glimmer suddenly fading from his eyes, and a strange, unreadable smile forming across his lips. I feel uncomfortable under the intensity of his gaze.

"That," he says simply, "might be the strangest thing I have ever heard."

There's no malice, no rudeness, in his voice, and I'm surprised, mostly because I agree with him.

"Yeah, it's pretty weird."

"But it's cute. Definitely cute."

Doan breaks our eye contact and reaches down into the water to pick up the cooler as my heart slams against my chest at those simple words. Damn him.

He passes the box to me a second time and I grip it harder now and manage to get it on board without meeting his eyes. I set it down just off to the side of the ladder and watch as he climbs aboard.

"We're just waiting on a few more people and then we can head out," he says. "I'll put this stuff in the fridge below deck. You can come see it if you want."

I don't say anything as I follow him down a narrow set of stairs and into a cramped kitchen. There's a single-burner stove, sink and microwave immediately to my left and a wide, tan leather wrap-around couch fills the rest of the small space.

"This is the galley," he says. He stops in front of a small mini fridge, the kind you expect to see in college dorm rooms, and kneels down, setting the cooler on the floor next to him. "Have a seat."

I wander -- okay, it takes me all of two steps -- over to the couch and sit on the section closest to the fridge. I watch as Doan carefully lifts the lid of the cooler to make sure lake water doesn't come sloshing out, but my eyes widen when I take in the rows and rows of beer cans inside.

I guess I'm not really sure what I expected when my 21-year-old brother asked me to hang out with him and his college friends on the Fourth of July, but somehow, drinking beer never crossed my mind.

I don't know why I thought Justin, of all people, would pack a cooler full of Diet Coke and Sprite to bring to Doan, of all people, but here we are.

When I look up at him, I see Doan staring back at me with an intense expression on his face, almost as if he'd known to watch for my reaction and didn't want to miss it.

I blink twice, trying to keep my face blank and relaxed.

Beer.

It isn't really a big deal at all -- even if I'm 18 years old and have still never taken a sip.

Plenty of people drink, and they do it all the time, and they turned out okay. But I still know it doesn't always happen that way. All of my friends back in Pennsylvania do it. I just -- I don't know. I guess I was always afraid that I'd be that person, the one who couldn't handle it, that something bad would happen to me the first time I drank. So I didn't.

But between my brother and Doan, I have a hard time imagining that I'll be able to avoid it here for long.

And I know Justin won't let anything terrible happen to me if I try.

"You good, Holls?"

I snap out of my thoughts and look at Doan, trying to paint a carefree smile on my face. "Fine. I'm fine."

He raises an eyebrow like he doesn't believe me, but says nothing as he starts placing beer cans inside the small fridge.

"So," he says, "I hope you have your bathing suit on under that dress."

I glance down at my outfit like I won't remember what I'm wearing if I don't look. "Of course I do. We're at the lake, aren't we?"

"Sure, but sometimes people forget," he says. "Or they want to stay on the boat. Which is lame."

"I've never been lame," I fire back.

"Okay, okay, you win," he says, holding up his hands in an 'I surrender' pose.

The cooler's empty now and Doan pushes himself to his feet and closes the door to the fridge.

"Let's get back on deck."

"Can you sleep on this boat?" I ask as we climb up the small staircase. I can't imagine that there's another space below deck than the one we're in now, and I don't see a bedroom anywhere.

"Yeah," he says. "The couch turns into a bed." He glances back at me over his shoulder. "Why? You interested in a slumber party?"

I blush immediately and feel the heat seep across my chest as I know my skin turns red. I quickly look away from him.

Damn him, damn him, damn him.

Doan chuckles to himself as he walks up the stairs and we emerge onto the deck. Justin and four other people I don't recognize have all come on board.

"Awesome! Everyone's here," Doan says, pumping his fist. "Grab a seat, Holls, and let's get out of here."

My brother sits in the passenger seat next to the wheel and everyone else has claimed a spot on a similar wraparound couch. Doan, I know, will drive the boat. I look around; there's really nowhere for me to go.

But that's when one of the two girls I don't think I've seen before springs to her feet and wobbles slightly in the white stiletto heels she's wearing, then hurries over to Doan.

She flings her wire-thin, tanned arms around his neck and kisses his cheek. "Hi, Doan!" she cooes. "It's sooo good to see you!"

He gives her a half-smile, then snakes his arm around her impossibly-tiny waist. "Hey, Allison."

He shoots a quick glance in my direction and I quickly try to pull myself together. I suddenly feel like I've been slapped -- all the blood rushes to my cheeks, the sting of the open palm across my face, the twisting of my stomach -- and it's stupid. It's all stupid.

"I'll go sit down," I mumble and hurry over to the now-empty spot on the couch.

The engine roars to life and after the boat starts moving, it feels safe enough to glance up from examining my cuticles. Justin's staring back at me, a look that's half-smug, half-sympathetic on his face, and I'm not sure I like what he's implying with that either. I try to return his gaze with a strong, carefree smile, but I'd be willing to bet it looks more like a grimace.

I force myself to keep my eyes from traveling back over to Doan and Allison, but that doesn't last long. I can't help it.

And it's like I've been slapped all over again.

I hate that I feel this way. I don't get why I feel like this. I shouldn't care. I didn't think I cared. But apparently I do.

Allison perches delicately on Doan's lap as he effortlessly guides the boat through the clear blue waters toward the middle of the lake. He's wearing sunglasses so I can't see his eyes, but his arm rests just to the side of her thigh, not making contact.

That, for some reason, feels like a small victory to me.

"Hey. I'm Joey."

The guy sitting next to me on the couch lazily leans over and holds out his hand. He's dressed in a flimsy white cotton T-shirt and blue swim trunks, has several days' worth of black stubble decorating his face, and I guess he's looking at me behind his gold aviators.

I smile at him and take his hand. "Holly. Justin's sister."

He nods. "Good to meet you," he says, and then he turns his attention away from me. I look at the other guy and girl to see if they'll introduce themselves, but the three of them start talking about a friend of theirs, so I tune out.

So much for that.

Justin's across the boat and Doan's clearly occupied, so I turn to my right and stare out over the water. The mountains glow red in the late morning sunlight, the warm rays seeping into my slowly-tanning skin the same way.

There are several islands littering the water, small ones with just some sand and trees and rocks, but big enough to spread out several towels and lounge around on. I wonder if that's in Doan's plans for today.

"This spot look good?" Doan calls out.

I glance over in time to see him jiggle his legs and Allison slides off them, a pout clouding her face.

Doan has slowed the boat down to a crawl in the center of the lake.

"Works for me," Justin says, and Doan nods. He cuts the engine and heads to the back of the boat to drop the anchor before he jogs down below deck. He's back a minute later juggling several cans of beer in his arms.

Justin and Joey immediately jump to their feet and go over to take them from him. He passes them each a can, then goes to Allison next. She looks at it for a second before accepting it. I watch, a growing sense of panic forming in my stomach, as he goes to the other girl and guy that I haven't been introduced to, and then starts walking over to me with just two left in his hands. One's for him.

The other, I know, is for me.

Why is this such a big deal? I'm 18. An adult. I could up and join the Army tomorrow. I can vote and drive a car.

So why does the thought of drinking a beer -- of drinking one little beer -- bother me so much?

Fear of the unknown, I guess. Or something like that, anyway.

It feels like Doan is walking extra slowly, but he finally stops in front of me and smiles, a warm, friendly smile.

He holds the can out to me.

"Want one?" he asks.

I don't sense pressure in his voice or that he'll ridicule me if I say no.

Most of me is relieved.

But part of me -- and it's a growing part -- kind of wants to say to hell with all my worries and try it. Worrying about things that might happen is like trying to light a candle in a thunderstorm. You can do it all you want, over and over again, and it never works the way you want it to.

I mean, what's the point?

I'm with Justin. I'm with Doan. And while Doan is probably dangerous in ways I can't begin to imagine, I've spent enough time with him lately to know he's not going to let me do anything too stupid if things get out of hand.

"Yeah," I say. "Okay."

He raises his eyebrows but says nothing as he passes one of the cans to me. I take it and hold onto it. He cracks the last can in his hand open and takes a long swig.

"Better," he says when he's done. "Much better."

I look down at the beer in my hand and open the tab. I don't have to glance at him to know that Doan's watching me the whole time.

Slowly, I bring the can to my lips. I sniff at it and try not to wrinkle my nose. A soft chuckle escapes Doan's lips but I don't pay any attention to him. And then without really thinking about it any more, I tip the can back and drink.

The beer is cool, but not cold. It doesn't really taste bad. I don't know what it tastes like. Certainly nothing I've had before.

I take another sip, then another. Before I know it, the whole can is almost empty.

"Slow down, tiger," Doan says, looking at me with an amused grin on his face. "Leave some for the rest of us."

I smile at him. "This isn't so bad."

"It's always easy in the beginning," he tells me.

"What, it gets harder to drinker?" I ask.

He shakes his head and grins. "No," he says. "Harder to stop."

I look him in the eye as I tip back and drain the rest of the beer.

"I feel fine," I tell him.

He shakes his head and laughs. "Give it a minute."

Justin wanders over to us then and claps Doan on the back with a loud thud. "What the heck is this? Corrupting my little sister?"

I grin innocently at him. "I told you he was a bad influence."

Justin shakes his head. "It's better this way," he says. "You need to drink before you go off to college."

I tense slightly at the mention of going to college and it's not long before I feel Doan's eyes on me, probing, remembering what I told him and no doubt wondering why Justin doesn't know.

Meanwhile, all I can think about is how unexpected it is that he remembers I said anything about it at all.

"Yeah," I say with a small, plastered-on smile. "You're right."

"Let me get you another," he replies, disappearing below deck, leaving Doan and me alone together once more.

"I don't want to talk about that," I say, refusing to meet his eye.

"Okay," he says. "We don't have to."

I look up at him. "Really?"

He nods. "Seriously? You're surprised that I'm not pushing you for not wanting to tell me something?"

I raise an eyebrow. "Did you forget the whole 'I really want to know who you are, Holly' campaign of yours? It was only last week."

He smiles. "That's different."

"Nope."

"Yeah, it is. Wanting to know who someone is and needing to know every last detail about them and their past and the decisions they make are totally different. I'm more interested in knowing why you don't want to go to college than I am in knowing why you haven't told your brother about it. That doesn't affect me."

I'm not sure I'm buying what he's selling but I've seen the galley and I know Justin isn't going to be down there all that long. The last thing I need is for him to overhear part of my conversation with Doan and get into this with him on the Fourth of July.

"Okay," I say, and Doan blinks twice. But when my brother walks up the stairs a few seconds later with three cans in his hands and passes me another beer, I see the understanding flicker in his eyes.

"Crafty one," he mutters under his breath.

"Don't get too crazy now," Justin says as I crack the tab open.

"When have you ever known me to get crazy?" I respond, and he laughs.

"Fair enough." He flips his sunglasses down over his eyes and holds out his can to me. "Cheers. Happy Fourth."

I clink my can with his, then Doan's, and the three of us drink. I notice the taste a little bit more this time, but I still don't really hate it. It's just sort of...there. And Doan's right. It goes down even easier.

Doan finishes his beer before I'm halfway done with mine and runs below deck to grab a few more. When he's polished them off, he grabs the bottom hem of his red T-shirt and pulls it over his head.

I can't keep my eyes off of him as I watch the fabric inch higher and higher up his torso. Each fraction of tanned skin makes my heart pump just a little bit faster.

The beer must be affecting me more than I thought. I vow to go slower on the next one.

"Who's ready to jump in?"

Allison looks over at him like he's crazy, but I stand and pull the sundress off over my head. It's hot out here in the blistering late-morning sun and a dip in the water sounds perfect.

"That's the spirit," Doan says when he sees me. He tosses two pink inner tubes over the side of the boat. "Come on, let's jump."

I slowly walk over to where he's standing. He climbs up onto the edge of the boat, then turns and extends a hand to me, and I immediately flashback to the time in the parking lot when he did the same thing to help me into the truck.

I didn't take his hand that time, but I find myself placing my palm in his now. And I only get a little bit of satisfaction knowing that Allison is right behind us to see it.

"Ready?" he asks. "On the count of three. One.."

I glance over at him and smile. I fight the urge to squeeze his hand. "Two."

He looks back at me. "Three. Jump!"

I spring off the small white edge of the boat and don't let go of his hand as I fall toward the calm blue water. Somehow our hands separate when we hit the water with a splash and I relish the feeling of the cool, refreshing water washing over me. When I can't hold my breath much longer, I swim up toward the boat.

Doan's already surfaced by the time I wipe water droplets from my eyes and look around. He's smiling at me as I smooth back my wet hair.

"Nice, right?" he asks.

Apart from his boat and several others littering the water, there's nothing surrounding me but miles of lake, red mountains and cacti. It's beautiful and natural and lovely, and I can't feel anything other than total bliss looking at it.

I'm startled out of my trance by the splash of an inner tube landing in front of me. Doan's climbing into his and I duck under the water and swim up through the center before hoisting myself through and letting my legs dangle over the sides.

I let out a small sigh.

It's perfect here, right now, in this lovely slice of desert, and I don't want to be anywhere else.

Doan paddles his tube over toward mine and loops a long white rope through the handle grips before tying them together, keeping our tubes attached.

I try to suppress my smile at being tied up next to him, and that only gets harder when I look up at the boat and see Allison glaring at us from her seat behind the wheel.

"Heads up!"

Justin tosses two beers down to Doan, who catches them with ease and passes me one.

"Thanks," I say, taking it and cracking open the tab.

It's hot out here, even in the cooler water, and I drink the cold alcohol greedily.

"You still feeling good?" Doan asks, lazily kicking at the surface of the water with the toe of his right foot.

I nod and smile at him from behind my sunglasses. "I feel great."

"Go easy with those, okay?" he says, pointing to the beer in my hand. "It's hot and you can't handle your alcohol."

I narrow my eyes even though he can't see it. "What makes you think I can't handle my alcohol?"

"Holls, please. This is the first time you've ever drank anything. I know what that's like, okay?"

I don't appreciate the smugness, the arrogance in his voice. "I'm fine."

"Don't get bent out of shape," he tells me, rolling his eyes. "I just want to make sure you're okay out here."

"Since when are you all sweet and concerned about me?"

"I keep telling you, I'm not a bad guy."

I feel the anger seep out of me. Maybe it's the beer catching up with me or maybe it's just that it's gorgeous here or maybe it's because I'm less hardened to the idea that Doan's a total jerk these days.

"I guess I'm going to have to start listening to you, huh?"

He shrugs, then takes a sip from his own can. "I mean, I personally think that's a great idea. But it's your funeral."

I look out over the water at the tiny sailboats littering the horizon. "I guess we'll see what you've got."

He raises an eyebrow. "What I've got?"

I nod. "We'll see how far off the track you steer me."

He laughs. "I promise not to steer you wrong, Holly Shaw. Scouts' honor. Besides, you really can't go wrong with me. You'll see."

I study his face, suddenly feeling myself growing more serious than I'd meant to, but I shake it off. "You were a boy scout?"

He shakes his head. "Nope. But it sounded like the right thing to say."

I don't say anything as I drain the rest of my beer.

"Hey, Justin," I call out. My brother turns around from his spot on the boat where he's been entertaining a very pouty-looking Allison for the past half hour. I wiggle the can in my hand before tossing it in his direction. "Catch."

He grabs it out of the air. "No more for you."

"What? Come on, one more."

Justin shakes his head. "No chance. It's about to hit you and then you'll be glad you listened to me."

I glare at him. "You don't know what you're talking about."

My brother exchanges an amused look with Doan.

"What?" Doan says with a grin. "I think it's cute. She's never had a drink a day in her life before but now she thinks she knows better than you and me."

I turn to him. "I know myself better than you know me. So there."

"So there?" Doan repeats. "Did you just hit me with a 'so there' and actually mean it? Yeah, Justin's right. You're definitely cut off."

I still don't feel any effects from the alcohol. I just feel...happy. My thoughts aren't swimming. I'm not slurring my words. I don't feel like I'm not in control of what I'm saying or doing. None of the bad stuff I'd been worried about is happening, but for some reason, Doan and Justin are being difficult about this, and I don't like it.

"Can I just get a beer please?" I call to my brother.

He shakes his head. "I'm not getting you one."

Then I'll get it myself." I put my hands in the water and begin paddling my tube toward the boat, but it's a lot harder with Doan tied to me, weighing it down.

"Don't look at me for help," he says, leaning back in his tube with his arms folded behind his head as though he's really about to enjoy watching me figure this out.

I stare at him for a few extra seconds before scooting to the edge of the tube then jumping down into the water. I swim over to the boat, climb up the ladder, smirk at my brother and march below deck to the mini-fridge where I find another drink.

When I emerge back into the sunlight, everyone's staring at me.

"Something wrong?" I ask without thinking about it. I'm surprised by my boldness. It's not like me. Allison and her friend both raise their eyebrows then look at one another. Justin grins, and the other two guys don't look interested at all.

"Holls, c'mere," my brother says, walking over to me and putting his arm around my shoulder. He guides me gently away from the others.

"What?" I ask.

He spins me around so that I'm directly facing him. "Slow down," he says. "We're going to be out here all night for the fireworks. You don't need to get drunk this minute."

I shake my head. "I'm not trying to get drunk."

"Well, that's what's going to happen if you keep going like you are."

I just roll my eyes. "I feel fine, Justin."

"Do what you want," he says. "But you're making a mistake."

I push past him and climb back down the ladder into the water before swimming to my tube with the beer in my hand. I swim up through the bottom and climb in, placing the can in the cup-holder built into the float.

Doan looks over at me. "Everything good?"

"Everything's just perfect."

I check out my surroundings one more time to shake off the icky feeling of the stupid confrontation with my brother and let out a happy, content sigh.

"Yeah," I mutter under my breath as I wiggle into a more comfortable position in the tube and let my eyes flutter closed behind my sunglasses. "It's perfect."

***

A freezing sheet of water splashes on top of me and I sit up with a start, forget where I am and immediately feel myself sinking underneath the water.

I flounder around for a few seconds before shaking off the groggy sleep and remember why I'm here. Fourth of July. Doan's boat. Floating in a tube. Everything's fine. I'm fine.

I swim toward the surface and break into the sunlight, expecting to feel the heat of the blazing desert sun warm my skin but it's chillier now than I remember it being earlier, and I wonder what time it is.

I look around. Doan's tube is empty but still floating tied to mine. I feel a wave of panic start to wash over me before I spin around and catch sight of the boat still anchored where we left it.

Everyone's on board.

I blow out a deep breath, hook the tube in the crook of my elbow and begin paddling toward the ladder.

"Well, good morning, sleeping beauty," Doan says when he sees me swimming over.

I glare at him. "My head hurts."

I don't understand the wide, self-satisfied smirk that slowly spreads across his face.

"I bet it does," he says. "Climb up. I'll get you some water."

I drag myself on deck and grab one of the dry towels from the stack resting near the back of the boat and wrap it around myself.

"Come with me," he says, jogging below deck.

I follow him, the pounding in my head seeming to get louder with every movement of my feet on the stairs.

Doan rummages around in one of the two small cabinets above the microwave while I slump down onto the couch. A few seconds later, he crouches down by my side with a plastic cup of water. He holds out two pills to me.

"Advil?" I ask.

He gives me a sweet smile and nods. "You look like you need it."

I swallow the pills in one try, drain the water and let out a sigh. "How long was I sleeping?"

He glances at the clock hanging above the stove. It's almost five now. "A couple of hours."

"And you didn't wake me?"

He shrugs. "I know what it's like to drink in the sun. Wipes you out. Sleep's good for that."

"I didn't even drink that much," I protest. "And I definitely didn't feel drunk."

"You probably weren't, but you were buzzed. And it's new to you." He smiles and pats my bare knee. "You'll get used to it, believe me."

I grimace, the thought of experiencing this kind of splitting headache again incredibly unappealing. "Or maybe not."

"Hungry?" he asks, getting to his feet.

"I could eat," I say, and I hear my stomach grumble loudly as I think about food.

Doan raises his eyebrows and laughs. "I'd say so. Come on, we're going to go dock over by one of the islands and grill."

We walk back above deck where everyone else is hanging out and talking and laughing. Allison, I notice, is now perched comfortably on my brother's lap, and I can only shake my head and chuckle quietly to myself.

I'm not sure where I should go as I stand here for a few awkward seconds by myself while Doan deals with the anchor. I happen to catch his eye (and definitely not because I'm staring at him) and he motions me over by the wheel with him once he's finished.

I'm also not sure why this fills me with such a smug sense of satisfaction, but it does, and all I really want to do is turn around and grin at Allison as I walk over to him.

He drops down into the seat, plays with a few gadgets on his dashboard and the engine roars to life. He swings the wheel and guides the boat in the direction of a small patch of land in the middle of the lake, barely big enough to be considered an island.

When the boat's cruising along comfortably, Doan looks over at me and pats his knee. I stare back at him blankly as he raises his eyebrow and chuckles.

"Okay, we're not there yet," he says in that infuriating but adorably unflappable voice of his. "Good to know."

"What?" I respond lamely.

He doesn't have to explain before it sinks into my still-thundering head that he'd been asking me to sit on his lap.

Duh.

I shake my head.

Sometimes I'm too clueless for my own good.

I hold a three-second debate in my mind. I can either awkwardly sit down without saying anything and make the situation even more ridiculous or I can crack a joke and hope he invites me a second time.

It doesn't take long for me to make a decision.

And of course I pick the more embarrassing of the two options.

I drop down onto his lap without a word, and I can hear his soft chuckle fill my ear that's suddenly a lot closer to his lips than it's ever been before.

Than I ever thought it would be.

Than I ever thought I wanted it to be.

But the funny thing is, I'm finding out that I sort of don't hate it at all.

The sky dims now as night falls. The air feels cooler, though it's still warm, but with my wet skin and hair, I shiver in the setting sun.

Doan must feel the vibrations coming off me because he wraps his arm that isn't piloting the boat around my shoulders and rubs some warmth back into my skin.

I feel the tingles of his touch hot on my skin and it's all I can do not to shiver again, but this time not from the dip in temperature.

We ride the rest of the way over to the island like this, with Doan's left hand lightly brushing against the exposed skin of my shoulder. I don't dare shift even an inch in either direction because I don't want his touch to end, even though I know it will.

It has to.

Doan slows the boat down to a crawl, then brings it to a complete stop in shallow waters. He jiggles his leg and I immediately get to my feet and wrap the towel around me tightly.

He drops the anchor first, then the ladder.

I turn to the galley steps and see Justin already coming up them with a small grill in his arms. The other guys come up with coolers and drinks and the girls have blankets in their hands. I'm just wondering how they all fit down there at the same time.

I also notice they've all changed out of their bathing suits and into shorts and sweats.

I look around for my bag and find it laying against the couch.

"Probably a good idea," Doan says, nodding as I pull out a pair of shorts and a sweatshirt. "I'll wait for you while you get changed."

I take the clothes down to the galley with me and slowly strip out of my still-wet bathing suit and change into a dry bikini. I toss my sweatshirt and shorts on, shove my feet back into my flip-flops and trot back up the steps, avoiding looking in the mirror hanging on the side wall at all costs.

"Ready?" Doan's standing over by the ladder when I get up to the deck. I walk over to him and he reaches out and gently brushes his hand against the small of my back as he guides me in front of him.

"You first," I tell him, and he gives me a funny look before he goes down the ladder, the last of the things we'll need for grilling dinner tucked neatly under one of his arms.

He gets down the ladder and stands in the shallow water, waiting for me. I turn to climb the short distance down.

As I'm climbing, my left foot lands on one of the rungs but my shoe must be wet from the lake or maybe it's just the ladder, I'm not really sure.

But all I do know is that I lose my balance first, my grip second, and my foot swings out from under me and I'm falling backward toward the very shallow water with a very hard, sandy, rocky bottom that isn't going to be too kind about catching my fall.

And just as I squeeze my eyes shut as tightly as I can to brace for impact, two strong hands reach out and grab my arms, steadying me. They pull me against Doan's solid, broad chest, my toes just dangling in the water as he holds me up.

"Son of a bitch," he mutters to himself as he eases me down and gently sets me in the water.

"What was that?" I ask, not sure I know exactly what just happened.

"You fell, I caught you," he says, that cocky, teasing smile back in his place on his face where I'm so used to seeing it now that it doesn't irritate me anymore.

It just feels like Doan.

"My hero," I tease, looking at him then frowning. "What happened to all the stuff you were carrying?"

"Dropped it to grab you," he says.

I look down into the water and sure enough, paper plates, cups and napkins float around my ankles.

"Oops."

Doan shrugs and smiles and turns to start walking toward the shoreline. We head up to the beach and join the others in easy silence.

Justin and Joey are working on lighting the grill while Allison hovers over my brother's shoulder, and I'm not sure what happened to the other two people whose names I still don't know.

"Got it!" Justin calls out triumphantly as a small flame shoots up. He and Joey lean back and rest on their calves in the sand, and when Allison plants a kiss on Justin's cheek, it's hard for me to keep from smirking.

But instead I just look around for Doan and find him standing near a palm tree maybe twenty feet away, watching me. I blush and immediately shift my gaze away.

"Do you guys need help with anything?" I ask, desperate for something to do to keep me busy.

My brother shakes his head. "We're good, Holls. Thanks."

"You can help me spread out the blankets," Allison pipes up, pushing herself to her feet and disentangling herself from Justin. "I don't know where Cam and Liz went, anyway."

I stare at her for a few silent seconds before nodding and following her a few yards away from the grill.

She hands me an end of one of the blankets and we shake it out then spread it on the sand. When I happen to glance up at her, she's staring back at me.

"So," she says. "You and Doan, huh?"

I shrug and place my end of the blanket neatly on the ground. "What about us?"

"You're a thing."

I smirk and shake my head. "No, we aren't."

But Allison just smiles. "I've known him for a long time," she says. "A long time. I've never seen him watch someone the way he watches you."

A small shiver prickles at the base of my spine. "How does he watch me?"

"Like he doesn't have any other choice."

I feel my cheeks start to grow warm as I think about this.

I'm not sure what it means, not even sure what I *want* it to mean. Doan isn't the kind of guy I'm interested in; I've said that from the beginning.

But what happens when things change?

Are they changing?

I don't know the answer.

I'm not sure I want to, either.

Allison spreads out her end of the blanket and smooths it out before getting to her feet and picking up the second.

"You look flustered," she observes, passing me part of it.

I shake my head as if that'll help me clear out the loud, buzzing thoughts battling around in me now. "Nah, I'm fine."

Allison lifts an eyebrow. "I'd believe you if I didn't know what Doan can do to a girl myself."

She's definitely grabbed my interest with that. "What's that supposed to mean?"

But Allison only grins like she has a secret only she knows and she isn't planning on sharing.

"If you have to ask, you haven't figured it out yet."

"You're freaking me out," I tell her, and I'm only half-kidding.

She waves a hand dismissively in my direction. "Don't worry," she says. "It'll be different with you guys. You'll see."

We finish spreading out the blankets then make our way back up to the guys gathered around the smoking grill in silence.

And I have no idea what to think.

***

"Those were so good," Allison says, putting her empty plate stained with ketchup on the sand next to the blanket. "Nice job, Doan."

He looks up from his burger. He's just taken a huge bite out of it and grins bashfully while he chews. Allison laughs and even I can't help but smile.

Doan just looks so cute sitting there like this, and I'm not happy that I'm noticing him this way now.

But I can't get Allison's words out of my head and I don't know what to make of it.

All I know is that I'm having a really hard time keeping my eyes off him tonight.

And if we're being honest, it's been like that since the day I saw him in Dad's pool.

He happens to look up at me in the glow of the fire Justin built before the food was finished cooking. I'm staring absently at him while I think. He catches my eye and winks ever so subtly -- there and gone before you know it, a gesture meant only for me.

Night has fallen completely over the lake now, the fire the only light we have, and I'm starting to wonder when we're going to head back home. Even with my nap earlier, I'm having a hard time keeping my eyes from fluttering closed.

"Glad you liked it," Doan says once he's finished chewing.

"Yeah, you killed it on the grill," Joey adds. "Nice job, bro."

"It's about that time," he says. "Hand me your plates."

"I can clean up," I say, scrambling to my feet. "You already cooked and brought everything out here."

I'm not sure why I do it, but I catch Allison's eye then and she's looking back at me with an amused, I-told-you-so smile on her face.

Great.

"You don't have to do that," Doan says.

I shrug but before I can say anything, Justin answers for me.

"Yeah, she does," he says. "It's just who she is. That's definitely our mom's side coming out."

I turn to Justin slowly and find him smiling hesitantly at me. But I'm just surprised he remembers that. I return his smile before collecting everyone's trash and tossing into one of the empty plastic bags near the grill.

When I'm done, I realize that only Doan is left on the blanket. He's watching me as I figure out that it's just the two of us now.

Alone.

I slow my approach as I get nearer to him, but I'm close enough to see the amused smile spread across his face.

"Where'd everyone go?"

"They left."

I shake my head. "Oh, is that what happened? Thanks for that."

He grins cheekily at me and the fire is bright enough to show the twinkle in his eyes.

"Allison and Justin decided to take a walk. I don't know where the others went."

I drop down onto the blanket, close enough to let him easily cover the distance between us but leaving enough space that it doesn't seem like I want him to.

"Fireworks should start soon," he says without moving.

"From where?"

He shrugs. "Whoever brought some on the water. I had some last year but we figured out pretty fast that it's easier to watch everyone else shoot them instead." He pauses, then chuckles softly. "Plus, Justin almost blew his hand off."

I laugh. "You know that isn't the first time he's done that."

Doan nods. "He mentioned that. You were still living here when that happened, right?"

"Yeah. My mom wouldn't talk to my dad for days."

"What happened there?" he asks, his voice quiet and serious.

"Where?" I ask even though I know exactly what he means.

"With your parents. And you and Justin. Why'd you move away? What's the rest of the story you wouldn't tell me before?"

I take a deep breath and absently twist my hair into a loose spiral.

"You know you do that when you're nervous," he says, nodding at my hair.

I frown and instantly let go of the twist. "No, I don't."

He raises an eyebrow. "Pretty sure you do."

I can hear the amusement in his voice but with Allison's words blurring my thoughts, I'm unnerved that he's noticed me do this enough to point it out.

And be right about it.

"Do you want to hear the story or not?"

"Sorry." He stretches out and rests his head on the blanket. "Tell me. From the beginning."

"I told you a lot of it already."

"I want to hear it again."

I take a deep breath. "You know my dad used to play pro baseball."

"Yep. For Arizona."

I nod. "Right. And for Colorado," I say. "He got traded there right at the deadline and went and played out the year. Me and Justin and my mom stayed here. We watched all of his games. I still loved baseball then because it was the only thing I really knew. I didn't really think anything of it. Of Dad going to live in Colorado for a couple of months. He would go and he would come back and everything would be fine. He was going to retire at the end of the season because he didn't want to live in Colorado permanently and he still had a couple years left on his contract. And he did come back."

I pause before continuing as I pick up handfuls of sand and let the grains run between my fingers.

"I just didn't expect him to come back with someone else."

Doan draws in a sharp breath. "Tanya?"

I nod. "Tanya. They met in Denver. She was a manager in the front office for the team or something. I don't know. I never wanted to listen to their story. Dad moved back with her and then he told Mom. She had no idea it was coming. She went to pick him up at the airport that day expecting her husband to come home to her. He told her in baggage claim."

Doan opens his mouth to say something but I shake my head.

"No," I say. "Don't. It happened a long time ago but it still sucked. I was mad at him. You can't even imagine. I didn't want to watch baseball. I didn't want to play it and so I didn't. I walked away, gave it up. And I did the same thing with my dad. When Mom wanted to get out of town and start fresh, I jumped at the chance to go with her. Everything out here just reminded me of Dad and of baseball. He was still a legend out here for what he did for the team. I didn't want to be Ron Shaw's daughter anymore. I just -- I don't know. I wanted to be Holly."

"And now you are," Doan says quietly.

I look up at him sharply, taken aback by his comment, but I feel a funny stirring in my stomach when he says it. I can't help but smile.

"Yeah," I say. "I am."

"She's pretty great, too," he goes on, but before he can continue, the first thunderous crack of fireworks fills the air, lighting the dark sky.

We look at one another without saying a word as the fireworks sparkle and explode faster and more frequently, lighting up the area around us.

And that's when I realize that I don't need him to say anything at all. He listened. And he understands. He might even understand me.

And that's enough.

I'm not sure if I close the gap between us or if he does, but without even really thinking about it, I'm suddenly pressed up against him and his lips touch mine and they're soft and sweet and gentle at first, questioning, asking if this is okay, and my head is spinning and all I know is that I want more of him.

More of Doan.

Who would've thought?

CHAPTER FOURTEEN

The day after Fourth of July brings another baseball game. I'm feeling a lot better about this one than I did before my first, and I can't help but be thankful I stopped drinking early yesterday afternoon.

I'm more relaxed now than I remember being since I first got to Arizona, and I don't really have to think too hard about what's causing it.

And I'm about to see him in a few minutes for the first time since he kissed me.

It's enough to make my stomach twist itself into knots that don't want to be untangled.

I pull my green Honda into a parking spot next to the baseball field. Justin had spent last night with Allison and wasn't home in time to drive me to the game, but I don't mind. It's nice to have a few minutes to myself to process everything that's happening.

Even if I'm still as confused as ever when I get out of the car. I grab my baseball bag and bat from the backseat and head over to our dugout. The other team isn't here yet, and hardly any of my teammates are, either.

But Dad is.

"Hey kiddo," he says when he sees me approaching. "How was your holiday?"

"It was good."

"Your brother treat you okay?"

"Justin's great, Dad."

"And how are you feeling about the game?"

I shake my head; I knew he couldn't keep baseball out of the conversation for very long.

"I'm not going to screw everything up again today," I say with a sigh as I begin digging through the bag for my glove. "Don't worry."

"I'm not worried about that." Dad says this like he's offended I thought it in the first place. "I want to make sure you're holding up okay."

"Well, I'm fine," I tell him. "I'm ready to play."

"Good," Dad says. "You can tell me if you have any concerns, you know."

I'm trying to decide how to respond when I'm saved by the unlikeliest of heroes.

"Hey, Coach." Doan and my brother walk down the steps of the dugout and over to us. "How's it hangin'?"

Doan looks over at me and winks. I smile, feel my cheeks color and immediately look down at the dirty rubber floor.

"It's hanging just fine, Doan," Dad says, and I try to choke back a laugh.

I quickly return my attention to my bag so I don't get myself in any trouble.

"Great to hear it, sir," Doan says cheerfully. "Hey, Holls, let's go toss a ball around and warm-up. You down?"

"Sure."

I slide my glove on over my hand. Dad's looking from Doan to me and back to Doan as if he can see that there are puzzle pieces here that need assembling but he isn't quite sure how they fit together yet.

And I want to get out of the dugout before he starts asking questions I'm not up for answering.

I jog up the steps and out into left field. Doan follows, tossing a ball back and forth between his bare hand and his glove.

"Hi," he says once we've gotten away from Dad and Justin.

I grin. "Well, hello."

"You good?" he asks, and I know he's talking about more than just the game.

"Never better."

He laughs, then throws the ball to me. "Thought your dad might be giving you a hard time."

It lands in my glove with a soft, easy thud. "No more or less than usual."

"So I didn't get to step in and save the princess."

"Just means you'll have to try again."

"I'm okay with this," he tells me. "Always like to find a damsel, even if she isn't in much distress."

I shake my head as I lob the ball back at him.

"So you ready for the game tonight?" he asks.

"Hope so. My coach seems to think I'll be in pretty good shape, though."

He nods. "Definitely. Remember, just relax and enjoy it and hit the pitch you want, not the one you get."

We throw the ball a few more times and by then, the rest of our team and our opponents have assembled on the field. Doan and I make our way back to the dugout where Dad's posted the line-up card for the evening.

He gathers us in just outside the dugout for a few inspirational pre-game words but I tune him out.

I'm not exactly sure he's one to be dishing out words of wisdom.

After the little huddle breaks apart, we jog out to our positions. I look for Doan on the pitcher's mound but Dave Durden is tossing warm-up pitches to the catcher instead.

I frown before remembering that Doan pitched in our first game and has tonight off. He'll be in the bullpen instead of on the dugout's bench with the rest of us.

Great.

The game begins and it's slow at first; not a lot of action comes my way and I find that I'm having a hard time keeping myself totally focused on the pitches and at-bats. I realize it's probably a good thing Doan isn't on the mound tonight -- I'm not completely sure I'd be able to keep my eyes off him if he was.

Dad has me batting eighth in the line-up, two spots below where he put me for the first game, but it doesn't matter to me. My job is still the same.

We're in the third inning before I get to take a crack at the pitcher. Mike Neese has just finished striking out while I'm taking practice swings in the on deck circle.

I step up to the plate and stare in at the pitcher. I adjust my stance the way Doan taught me at the batting cages and get ready to wait for the ball.

The pitcher shakes his head twice before settling on a pitch with his catcher.

I wait. He winds up. His leg goes up. His arm pulls back. He pitches himself forward. The ball comes out of his hand. It flies in toward me. I recognize the curveball

right way, like it's coming at me in slow motion. I got this.

It's hittable. A perfect pitch. The one Doan was

always telling me to hope for.

I wiggle the bat above my head once, then

prepare to make contact. I smack the ball as hard as I can; I

feel it hit the end of my bat, heavy and hard, the weight of

the impact pushing down on my hands. The ball flies out

toward centerfield. I release my bat and start running for

first base, then second.

I make it safely, the ball arriving in the second

baseman's glove a few seconds after my foot touches the

bag.

I hear a few faint cheers and claps from the

stands and maybe the dugout.

A sense of relief washes over me even though I

haven't really done anything.   At least I'm on base. At

least I haven't forgotten baseball completely. Maybe it can still be a real part of me after all.

Because the thing is, the more I'm around it, the more I can't pretend I haven't missed it all these years, no matter how much I wish it wasn't true.

I force myself to pay attention as Cam Cooper comes up to bat with one out and me on second. He takes the first two pitches as strikes, watches the third land way up and outside and smacks at the fourth.

It trickles harmlessly to the first baseman who steps on the bag and makes the easy out. I stay put on second as my brother, the lead-off hitter, comes back up to the plate. Justin's already had one hit today in his first at-bat.

I'm hoping he can get another so I'll get to score a run.

I know scoring a run here isn't going to make me a hero. It's just the second game. But it might make me feel a little bit better about how baseball fits into my life.

Justin waits for the ball. He stares at the pitcher with an intensity I've never seen from him before, the eye black darker under his eyes than anyone's else.

He doesn't waste any time; he swings at the first pitch he sees. It's gone. I already know it. It flies back, back, back, way back. I watch, standing about halfway between second and third base to make sure, but I already know.

Sure enough, it flies over the outfield wall and rests easily in the grassy field behind us.

I clap my hands twice as I round third and head for home. And when my feet touch the plate, I let out a small sigh of relief. I know it wasn't my work that got us the run -- I haven't stolen a base or driven in the run, but at least I crossed the plate.

That counts for something to me.

I scored. I'm back. Baseball is back in my life.

**

Justin and I have scored our team's only two runs -- the only two runs of the entire game -- by the time the last inning rolls around. The Anthem Antlers are down to their final three outs and they have to score at least twice or the game's over.

Dave Durden isn't on the mound anymore. Dad's bringing in Doan to pitch the ninth and save the game for us.

I'm surprised by the move. Doan's never said anything to me about wanting to pitch in relief before, but I'm sure Dad has his reasons. He trusts Doan to get the job done.

I've been focused on the game, hardly thinking of Doan at all until he trots out onto the mound in his tight white baseball pants. I see the silver chain of his dog tags peeking out from the collar of his shirt, a reminder of the time I saw him at Dad's pool more than a month ago.

I have to laugh to myself, thinking about how quickly things can change even when it's the last thing you think you want. How maybe we don't even know what's best for us anyway.

Doan's ready. The first batter stares at him. It's an easy out; he flies out behind the catcher on the first pitch. We're just two outs away now from getting the win.

No sweat.

The next batter is up at the plate but I don't watch him. I watch Doan, every movement of his arms, legs, his whole body as it works in perfect unison to deliver a perfect pitch.

Doan stares in at the catcher who signals the call between his legs and Doan nods, then delivers.

The batter hits a slow groundball and it's coming right at me but I don't see it. I don't know what's happening until it's too late and the ball bounces between my legs and trickles into the grass behind me.

The batter reaches first base before I can throw the ball.

It never should have happened.

Groans fill the air and I feel my cheeks flush with hot, stinging shame. I've been so proud of what I've done today and now this. An error, no doubt, charged to my name.

My fault.

At the worst possible time.

I catch Doan's eye as I pound my fist into my glove. He smiles calmly, shaking his head, as if telling me not to worry about it, as if telling me that I have to forget it happened and have a short memory.

He's right, but I feel bad, except Doan's on the mound, and if anyone can fix it, I know it's him.

The next batter strikes out looking -- three pitches, three strikes. I sigh with relief. We've got this.

Everything's going to be fine.

What I hope is the last batter approaches the plate then.

He works his way to a three-two count and Doan stares in, ready to deliver the final strike and get the out.

The pitch flies in. The batter swings and the sickening crunch of baseball meeting wood fills the field. I watch as our center fielder gives chase; he's going back, back, back, just like when Justin hit his home run.

But now it's just dread in me because I know where this ball is going to end up and then it's flying over

Tommy's outstretched hands and lands tauntingly just beyond the fence.

A home run.

And not just a home run, but a two-run home run. All because of me. The game is tied.

It isn't lost on me that I'm going to be batting in the now-necessary bottom of the inning.

Doan gets the next batter out with ease. But it's enough damage for nausea to fill my stomach and keep me from wanting to go back out onto the field.

But I have to.

I can't meet my teammates' eyes in the dugout between half-innings and not even Dad comes over to talk to me.

Not that I'd take him all that seriously anyway.

But Doan's in the dugout now that he pitched and he finds me as soon as he can. He pulls me aside into the corner and puts both hands on my shoulders and looks into my eyes.

"Don't beat yourself up over this, Holls," he says. "Don't do it. I know you. Let it go."

I shake my head. "I can't."

"Well, that's too bad. You're going to have to find a way. It's up to you now."

"I'm sorry I ruined it for you."

"You didn't. The home run's on me."

"But it would've just been one run if not for me."

"Doesn't matter," he says. "I still threw the home run pitch after your mistake. It's still my fault. Don't think about it. Stop thinking about it."

"I can't."

"You have to."

"I have to win this."

"Don't think like that," he tells me. "You have to relax. Remember what I told you."

I stare at him. He's looking back at me like he needs me to believe him, to listen to him, to trust him.

"Do what I told you," he says. "Trust me."

"Trust you," I repeat under my breath, and I think how crazy it is to hear these words coming from him and how it's even crazier that I do.

After everything we've been through, after the very first day we met, here I am, hanging on his every word, believing his every word, and needing to hear from him that he thinks I can do this.

"You've got this, Holls. And even if it doesn't work out, it's just the second game. We can't lose here. Not in this inning."

I nod and grab my bat from its cubby.

Doan reaches in and pulls out my helmet. He smiles, glances around once and quickly bends down and brushes a kiss across my lips. I smile despite the nerves fluttering around in my stomach. He places the batting helmet over my head and taps the brim once.

"Go get 'em," he says to me.

I'm batting second. Mike Neese stands at home plate while I take a few half-hearted swings in the on-deck circle.

But I'm watching the pitcher as he gets ready to deal. Strike one. I shake my head, my fingers balling up into a nervous fist at my side.

Come on, Mike, get this hit.

The tense energy is palpable throughout the field, radiating off of both benches. I'm surprised how much I care about this summer league game.

The next pitches come in.

Strike two.

I can't keep a frustrated sigh from slipping out between my lips.

Mike holds up his hand to the umpire to call time out and steps out of the batter's box. He takes a few aggressive practice swings as if all he's thinking about is hitting a home run.

He steps back in, squares up and waits.

And that's when he does something that surprises everyone. The pitch comes in and he quickly switches up to a bunt.

A perfect bunt.

A strange time for it but it slowly, slowly, slowly trickles down the third baseline.

Mike's a fast runner, and by the time the infielder scoops up the ball and fires it to the first baseman, he's already crossed the bag.

He's safe.

Unconventional, but it works. A small smile flickers at the corner of my lips.

Until I realize it's my turn.

My walk to the batter's box feels a little bit like a funeral procession. My legs barely want to move, like they're tied down with weights, but I force myself to home plate.

This is what I want.

I want to be a baseball player.

This is the moment to take it.

And maybe that's the difference between people who like something and people who love it. When you love something, you'll do anything to have it, and failing isn't an option.

The pitcher looks in at the catcher's signals but I refuse to look anywhere other than his eyes until he throws the ball.

And when he does, it's low and outside for ball one. I hear a few encouraging calls and claps behind me.

"Alright, Holly, alright! Take that pitch."

"Come on, Holls! You got it."

I wait for the next one. It's going to be a strike but I think back to what Doan said. I don't like this pitch, I don't want this pitch, and it isn't mine. Strike one.

But that's okay.

I'm waiting for my pitch, the one I can hit, the one I want to hit, the one that comes sailing in at me whistling my name and only my name.

I know it'll come.

And there it is, on the very next throw.

I swing my arms back, bring the bat around and watch the ball fly out and over the infield.

It isn't a home run but it might be good enough. I take my eyes off the ball and run as hard as I can and I hope Mike is doing the same.

When I round second base, I see the left fielder has just picked it up. I look for Mike. He's halfway between third and home.

And with the left fielder just now throwing the ball in, he's going to make it. We're going to score. We're going to win!

I don't bother to keep running. As Mike crosses home plate before the ball and the game ends, I stop where I am and smile.

It's a strange smile. It's relief, and a little bit of sadness at having lost this game for so long, but mostly I'm just happy to have it back.

My teammates stream onto the field to celebrate. Doan finds me immediately, like I knew he would.

He wraps me up in a hug and kisses my cheek.

"I told you," he whispers into my hair.

I pull back from him and press my lips hard against his.

"I don't know how you could think I'd do it," I murmur back.

"Because I believed you could," he says. "And maybe it's time you start believing, too."

CHAPTER FIFTEEN

Two days later Justin decides he wants to have a pool party in Dad's backyard. Most of the guys from the team are coming. I know Doan will be here and I haven't seen him since the game.

He mentioned grabbing beers and burgers but I wanted to spend last night working on my music and see if I could finish that one song I could never find the right ending to.

But I still can't.

I'm up in my bedroom staring out over the valley when the door bell rings. I drag myself out of bed, pull on my red bikini and cotton dress and head down to the pool.

Justin and Allison are outside with Dave Durden and Mike Neese and a couple of girls I don't know. I say hello to everyone, glance around and realize Doan still isn't here.

I head into the pool house to grab some towels, spread them out on a lawn chair and flop down on my back, letting my eyes close behind my sunglasses as I listen to the soothing sound of the waterfall hitting the pool.

I'm not sure how long I doze off for, or even if I do, but when I come to it's because someone's talking to me.

"Hope you've got your sunscreen on."

I smile before I open my eyes. "I might need to re-apply." I let my eyes flutter open and grin at Doan who's standing in front of me with a bottle of sunscreen in his hands just like I knew he would be.

"I think I can help out with that," he says. "Flip over."

I turn onto my stomach and feel Doan's weight pressing down on the lawn chair as he gets on it with me.

I listen for the pop of the sunscreen tube and hear him squirt the lotion into his hands. I realize I'm holding my breath in anticipation of feeling him putting it on me.

Doan's warm, strong hands spread the sunscreen out across my back as he rubs it into my shoulders before working his way down lower and lower, making sure not to miss a spot, covering every inch with his rough pitcher hands.

I try not to shiver when he reaches my lower back.

He stops, puts more lotion in his hands and continues onto my legs. I feel his touch on every inch of my burning skin.

He lingers for just a bit and then I hear the disappointing sound of the tube closing and the chair springs back up once his weight no longer pushes down on it.

"Thanks," I say, turning back over. "Can I have that please?"

I'm not about to ask him to lotion up my front with my brother and our teammates hanging around. He grins and wiggles his eyebrows at me as if he knows exactly what I'm thinking, then passes the bottle to me.

He sits down on the lawn chair next to mine and watches as I cover the rest of me in sunblock.

"Let it soak in," he says. "Then you and me have a date with the water slide."

"Deal," I tell him.

He smiles and leans back, propping himself up with his elbows. "Not such a bad set-up you've got here."

I shrug. "Yeah, it's okay. But it's still my dad's."

"Right," Doan says. "And he's still your dad."

I look over at him sharply. "What's that supposed to mean?"

He shakes his head. "Nothing. Nothing."

"No," I say, sitting up and pushing my sunglasses onto the top of my head. "It's definitely something."

"Family is still family even when you don't want them to be."

"I never said I don't want him to be my dad." I'm mad now; I don't like the direction he's taken this conversation. Not today. Not after what I told him at the lake the other day.

"I guess that's true," Doan says. "But you don't seem to think of him like your dad."

I stare at him. "This isn't your place."

He seems to realize he's gone a little too far. "Hey, hey," he says, holding up his hands as if he's surrendering. "Sorry, you're right. I shouldn't have said anything. It's just hard for me sometimes. I don't think people really appreciate what it's like to have a family. And I don't necessarily mean you."

Something clicks in my head; this isn't the first time he's said something like this to me.

But I don't want to talk about this anymore.

"Water slide?" I finally ask.

He looks at me for a second or two with an unreadable expression in his eyes.

"Okay," he says at last, his voice friendly and normal and happy once again. "Let's do it."

I get up off my chair and walk over to the steps hidden behind the giant cluster of rocks.

Doan follows. We get up to the top of the slide and I feel weird around him after what just happened but he smiles at me like nothing's the matter at all.

So maybe it isn't.

I stand at the top of the slide, my arms pressing down onto the sides as I rock back and forth to get some momentum.

"What are you doing?" Doan says from behind me, and before I can turn to explain it to him, I feel two strong hands on my bare back and my feet shoot out from underneath me and I'm tumbling down the slide without even knowing what's happening.

And then I'm flying off the edge of the slide and hit the water with a splash. I barely have time to plug my nose before my head goes under. I twist around for a second, orienting myself, before kicking my way to the surface and swimming over to the ledge.

I wipe my eyes and blink twice.

"What the heck was that?" I yell as Doan grins at me from the top of the slide.

"Too slow!" he calls back before disappearing around a corner.

Seconds later, he flies off the slide, then swims over to me.

I whack his arm when he's within striking distance. "Not cool."

He waves his hand dismissively. "Eh, it was funny."

I slid off the edge and swim around in front of him. Before he can realize what's happening, I'm grabbing onto his legs and pulling him toward me. The weightlessness the water adds to his body makes it easy to yank him off the ledge and dunk him before he has a chance to react.

I hold him down for just a few seconds before letting go and swimming toward the opposite end of the pool.

By the time he splutters to the surface, I'm already far away.

"Oh," he says in a low voice, shaking the water off his hair and letting his eyes linger on me. "It's on now."

He springs forward and swims toward me and I shriek and stand up on the ledge. When he reaches me, I quickly jump out of the pool where he can't touch me.

"Cheater!" he exclaims. "So lame."

"All's fair in love and war," I tell him, and he doesn't respond for a few seconds.

He just stares at me, and my heart's thumping inside my chest all funny and weird all of a sudden, and I'm sure I'm reading too much into it, but I can't help it.

"You're right," he says at last. "Let's see what you got."

I glance around and notice that Justin and several other people are watching us. My brother's got that twinkle in his eye, the one I'm so used to seeing from when we were kids and he was about to suggest we do something that'd eventually get us in trouble with Mom and Dad.

"Water fight!" Justin shouts out before cannon-balling into the pool, soaking everyone he'd just been standing with.

Some of the girls shriek but the others jump in and within a second, Justin and Dave and Allison and another girl are engaged in chicken fights.

I realize with a start that I've taken my eyes off Doan for way too long. I scan the pool and don't see him anywhere.

Damn.

It's like he's the spider again.

And right now, I feel like I've stumbled into his web.

As I consider my next move, I realize that the answer is in the pool house and I hurry over to it, trying to sneak through the door unseen. There's no guarantee we'll have them but if I know my brother at all, they'll be here. I let it close quietly once I'm inside so I'll hear it if someone tries to get in behind me.

I root around through several plastic storage boxes until I find exactly what I'd been looking for.

I pick up the two mega-sized super-soaker water guns and smile. Doan'll be at my mercy in no time.

As I head to the back of the pool house to fill them with water from the hose, I'm hit with memory after memory of summers in Arizona in our old house, with my old family, before all of this.

We'd had a modest pool, definitely no pool house or rock-adorned water slide or mountain-side view, but it had been perfect for the four of us.

And it probably still would be, if we still had those lives.

They aren't the same water guns my dad had come home with that summer night one July almost 12 years ago, but they're close enough for me to remember it all.

I can still see the excitement on Justin's face, can still feel the amused mock disapproval of my mom's stare, can still picture the unbeatable little-boy smile of my dad.

We'd gone outside that night even though it was close to my bed time, filled those guns up and spent hours running through the yard, spraying each other. Mom and I had teamed up against Dad and Justin. Girls versus boys.

We were a real family then.

It's been so long since I could say that I almost forgot it was ever true at all.

And for years, memories like that had done nothing but refuel my anger at my father. But now? Today? Holding these water guns in this new life I stumbled onto not by choice but out of necessity?

I don't feel mad anymore.

I don't even feel sad that it's no longer the way it used to be.

No, for the first time, I just feel calm. At ease. There's nothing bad about these memories, and nothing bad about the way they make me feel.

With the weight of this in my hands, I peek my head around the back door. There's no sign of anyone.

I creep over to the hose, crank it on and quickly fill the water guns. When I'm done, I put one in each hand and slide over to the edge of the pool house, suddenly enjoying the feeling of being some kind of secret agent ready to take on the enemy.

Ready to take on Doan.

I stick my head around the corner and move forward. When I get to the edge of the pool house that faces the water, I try to casually walk away from the building even with the giant super soakers in my hands.

I stand easily behind a lounge chair, using the back of it to hide the guns as best I can.

And that's when I see him.

Doan's sitting on the opposite side of the pool with his legs dangling in the water, watching the two separate games of chicken going on in the shallow end in front of him.

I don't think he's seen me yet.

Perfect.

I walk over the long way, trying to keep out of his line of sight as best as possible, and when I'm almost directly behind him, I get the soakers prepared in my hands for maximum impact.

I walk up, practically on tiptoes, stop, aim and fire.

Water spurts out the ends of both of them, soaking his hair, his back, his shorts.

He turns around in surprise but that only ends with him getting a faceful of water and me getting the giggles.

"What the -- ?" he gurgles, wiping frantically at his face.

I'm smiling as I pull down on the trigger, launching another stream of water at him.

I stand here grinning, watching him struggle, until I realize both the guns are out of water, and he's suddenly no longer being bombarded.

He seems to realize it at the same time I do.

I shriek and take off running and don't stick around long enough to see if he scrambles to his feet and comes after me.

But when he grabs my ankles and tackles me into the grass a few seconds later, I have my answer.

The water guns fly out of my hands with impact and I expect him to take off after them and use my own weapons against me, but instead he's almost sitting on my stomach and starts tickling me relentlessly.

"Stop!" I shriek through my laughter. "Stop!"

"Oh, you want *me* to stop?" he says. "After that? I don't think so."

I'm struggling to find the air to talk. "You'll -- regret -- it," I manage to choke out between laughs. "Stop!"

"Nope!" He gleefully continues to tickle me, so I do what any girl in my situation would -- I lift my leg and kick him.

Not hard, of course, but enough to startle him and get him to just stop tickling already!

And when he does, I wiggle out from under him, manage to get my hands on one of the water guns and take off running back to the hose to fill it again, cursing myself for leaving the second for him.

It's quiet -- too quiet -- once I've re-filled mine, and I find myself creeping over to the edge of the pool house once again.

I stick my head around the side of the building and BAM!

That's when I get a face full of water.

"Gotcha," Doan whispers.

I cough, and before I can retaliate, he pulls the second gun out of my hands.

"Truce?" he asks.

I blink the water out of my eyes and glare at him. "Truce."

He grins. "Not bad," he says. "For a rookie."

"This isn't over," I tell him. "Not by a long shot. You know the whole thing about winning the battle but not the war. That's this."

"I hope it isn't," he says. "Come on, let's put these back for now."

I follow him into the dark pool house and over to the storage bins where I found the water guns.

"You fight dirty," he tells me, putting them inside.

"It's like I told you before -- "

"All's fair in love and war," he cuts in. "I know. I like the way you think."

I smile at him, and he takes a step toward me, and it's only then that I realize how close we already are, how much closer each movement he makes brings him to me.

And how every inch makes it just a little bit harder to breathe.

My heart slams against my chest as Doan looks right at me, and it's hard to see him because of the darkness but he's still somehow clear to me.

And then I feel his hands on my bare shoulders, hot and blistering. There's nothing gentle about his touch this time.

The only thing that feels the same as it did when he put his hands on me at the lake is that I can't think about anything other than his skin on mine.

He lowers his head and then his lips find me, hungry and searching, and I'm almost stunned at how much he seems to want me.

And how there's nothing sweet about his kiss.

His hands roam down my back and I wind my arms around his neck, using my hands to comb through his hair and pull him down closer to me, wanting to feel his lips pressed harder against mine.

I feel his mouth wander off my lips as he presses light kisses against my cheek before tilting my chin back and trailing a string of kisses down my neck, exploring more of me.

And I'm shocked at how badly I want him to keep going.

I'm so caught up in Doan that I almost don't hear the door to the pool house creak open, but the stream of light suddenly blazing inside sends me scampering away from him.

We both look up, startled and maybe feeling a little bit guilty.

"There you are," Justin says, looking from Doan to me and back to Doan. His voice is normal, his facial expression the same. He doesn't seem to realize what he's just interrupted. "Come back outside, we need a new team for chicken fights."

Doan and I look at one another, and I try to imagine calmly sitting on his shoulders in the pool after what just happened, and I can't do it.

But Doan just smiles. "Sure, we're in."

And he walks right out of the pool house without a glance in my direction.

Justin smiles at me and holds the door open as I pass by him.

"I told you," he says when I'm about a foot in front of him.

I turn around. "Told me what?"

He raises an eyebrow. "That you'd eventually learn to like Doan."

CHAPTER SIXTEEN

This weekend is the team's annual trip to California for a round-robin series with a league near Los Angeles that's just like ours in Phoenix.

Things are still good with me and Doan; we'd never gotten another moment alone to continue what we started in the pool house, but he'd stolen kisses from me here and there during practice and our only game during the week.

I pull into the parking lot of one of the local high schools where Dad's arranged for us all to leave our cars over the weekend while we're in California. A yellow school bus -- the kind I haven't set foot on since eighth grade -- waits along the curb.

Doan's black pick-up truck is already in the parking lot, and I can't help but think about how weird it is that the sight of it makes me smile now instead of making me mad.

I never expected Doan and I to end up where we are today, and I have no idea where we're going, but every day makes me a little bit more excited to get there.

There's something about him.

And, okay, maybe there always has been. I can't pretend I didn't feel some kind of pull toward him the very first time I saw him.

It's like my mom would always tell me before she married the count and moved to Italy: Plans are a nice idea, a guideline that you hope will get you where you want to go, but they hardly matter. You're going where the universe wants to take you, whether you like it or not, whether you see it or not.

That's how she ended up living in an Italian castle in Sicily, anyway.

And it's why I'm about to hop on a rickety old school bus with my dad and a bunch of baseball players.

Dad and most of the team are already on the bus when I climb on board. Doan stands up from a seat near the back and waves to me. I make my way back toward him.

"Hey," I say, dropping my bag on the floor next to his and leaning down for a quick kiss. "Thanks for saving me a seat."

He smiles. "I can think of worse people to be stuck next to on a five-hour bus ride."

"I guess I'll take that as a compliment."

Before he can say anything, Dad calls us to attention and does a quick roll-call to make sure everyone's present before the bus rumbles out of the parking lot. We're due to reach our hotel in Los Angeles just before nine o'clock tonight. We've got one game tomorrow and another Sunday morning before we leave.

The rest of the time is ours.

And I'd be lying if I said I wasn't excited to explore California with Doan at my side.

The first hour of the ride is mostly silent with people nodding off or talking quietly to each other. Doan had his head resting against the window, while I stared down at my song notebook, still trying to come up with the right answer for the song I can't seem to end.

When the bus hits a particularly nasty pothole on the freeway, Doan's head smacks into the window and startles him awake.

"You okay?" I ask as he looks around, trying to shake the sleep off and figure out where he is.

He looks over at me, confusion turning to happiness. "Hey you," he says. "Good morning."

I grin. "Morning, sleepyhead. Nice snooze?"

He nods and stretches his arms over his head, and I can't keep my eyes from drifting to the small sliver of tanned lower-body skin that peeks out between the hem of his shirt and the waistband of his jeans.

"Hey," Justin, who's been sitting behind us, leans over the back of the seat and looks at us. "We've still got like three hours to go. What do you say we play a round of Truth or Dare?"

"Seriously, bro?" Phil Allen asks. "There's one chick on the bus and she's with Doan and you wanna play that?"

My brother shrugs. "You got a better idea?"

Phil pauses, then shakes his head. "Nope."

"I'm down," Doan says, looking at me. "Holls?"

I think about it for a second before shrugging. "Sure. Okay."

"I've never backed down from a dare," Doan brags, and I smile and roll my eyes at him.

"We'll see about that."

"Sweet!" Justin looks pumped, then gathers the rest of the guys sitting near us and fills them in. They all agree because the next thing I know, there's a decent-sized group of guys all awkwardly hanging out of their seats, forming a misshapen circle in the aisle, kind of like we used to on middle-school field trips.

"I'll go first," Justin says. "Phil, give me something."

Phil looks up, startled. "Uh, I don't know."

My brother rolls his eyes. "Well, think of something."

"Truth or dare."

"Dare," Justin says with a smile.

Phil hesitates, then looks around for help that isn't about to come as everyone sits there trying to come up with a dare for themselves whenever it's their turn to challenge someone.

"Okay," he says at last, looking unsure of himself. "I dare you to moon the window."

Justin raises an eyebrow. "That's the best you got? Fine."

I can't help but chuckle but I look away as my brother drops his basketball shorts and presses his ass cheeks against the bus window.

"This long enough?" he asks.

"Yes, please!" I cry out, and Doan grins and pokes me in the shoulder.

"Sorry that can't be me," he whispers into my ear, and I can only laugh.

Justin finishes, then eyes Doan. "Okay," he says. "You. Truth or dare?"

I freeze as I realize this order means that Doan'll be the one to give me my orders, and I'm not sure how I feel about that.

On one hand, I don't think he's going to ask me to do something like flash the bus, but on the other, there's still that element in our relationship (or whatever it is) where we like to make fun of each other.

I can definitely see him having me do something a little crazy and embarrassing.

"Dare," Doan says without hesitation.

"Give up your cigarettes for the week," Justin says equally fast.

An eerie silence fills our small part of the bus. I've only asked him about smoking that one time, but even I know that what Justin's just suggested isn't about to go over so great.

"What?" Doan finally chokes out.

"You heard me," Justin says, the challenge clear in his voice and his eyes. "And what was it that you said before? You've never backed down from a dare, right?"

Doan shakes his head. "That's low, man."

"Maybe," my brother says. "But those are the cards."

"I'm not doing that," he says. "I can't."

"Yeah, I think you can," Justin replies, and I can't help but wonder why my brother chose this moment to turn a light, fun game of Truth or Dare into something it isn't supposed to be.

The two stare at one another, no blinking, no movement, each daring the other to back down first.

It takes me a minute before I realize I'm holding my breath.

But mostly I just really want to know what the heck has Doan so riled up about his cigarettes.

Doan blinks first. "You're really serious about that?"

Justin nods.

"Thought you were better than that, man," Doan says. He picks up his duffel bag, climbs over me and walks up to the front of the bus.

I can hear the sound of his metal bat hit the side of the bus when he tosses his bag into an empty seat.

No one says a word.

"Um," I finally say at last. "I guess that's it for that, huh?"

The guys all mutter and nod and turn their attention back to their seats. I get up on my knees and lean over the back of the chair.

"What is going on?" I ask my brother.

Justin just shakes his head. "You have to ask him."

I bite down on my bottom lip. "You know what?" I hiss, trying not to cause a scene. "I'm tired of that. I'm tired of you always defending him or telling me to trust him or making some reference to some story he has and then never telling me what's going on. You started all of that, Justin, and it wasn't like it was some private conversation I walked in on. You did that publicly, now you tell me what the heck is going on here."

"I won't do that," he says.

"Why not?"

Justin shrugs. "Because I wouldn't want someone to do that to me."

"Oh, but you'd want them to essentially hint at some giant issue during a friendly bus game?"

My brother sighs. "Maybe that wasn't my most brilliant idea," he says. "But I made my point."

"And what is your point?"

"Give it up, Holly."

I turn around and slump back in my seat. I know --
- and I've always known -- that there's something about
Doan, some part of his story that I never got and that I may
never get. I'd almost accepted this, even, but when it
constantly gets thrown around and it clearly bothers him
this much -- it's not something that I'm okay with.

Without really thinking about it, I stand and
march to the front of the bus where he's sitting and drop
down into the seat next to him.

"What's the deal?" I ask.

He looks over at me and blinks. "Huh?"

I roll my eyes. "Enough," I tell him. "I know, I
know. Not every story is meant to be told. That's fine. But
you guys can't keep talking about things like this in front of
me if you and I are ever going to work out."

Doan stares at me without saying anything for a
long time. I don't let myself break eye contact even though

I want to look away. He needs to know I'm serious about this.

"Didn't you find out most of it, anyway?" he asks.

I shrug. "I don't know. Did I?"

"My brother," he says. "In Iraq. He used to smoke all the time." He shakes his head. "Actually, he smoked before he went overseas. He'd offer me a cigarette here or there but I didn't do it much. When I did, we had some of the best talks we've ever had over a smoke and a bottle of beer in the backyard." A small smile dances on the corners of his mouth. "So when he left, it was kind of a way to get that back, you know? I missed him."

Yeah.

Yeah, I do know.

Because it's the exact same feeling I had in the pool house the other day holding those super soakers.

Without saying anything else to him, I lean over and rest my head on his shoulder.

He strokes my hair absently and the next time I look up, we're in California.

***

I have my own hotel room -- Dad and I are the only ones without roommates -- and I'm a little nervous about it. Doan and I have plans to go snorkeling this morning but I'm afraid the guys will grab him before I wake up and I'll be stuck on my own all day.

But when I wake up and check my phone, I already see a text from Doan asking me to meet him in the lobby in half an hour.

I smile as I hop into the shower.

Part of me finally feels like Doan and I are completely on the same page. I feel like I understand him now from that short, simple conversation yesterday. He misses his brother in Iraq.

I know I'd miss Justin if he got deployed to a war zone. I bet I'd do some pretty weird things, too, waiting for him to come home.

So because of all that, I'm a little more willing to overlook some of Doan's...less-positive tendencies.

And, okay, part of it is the way he makes my stomach twist when he looks at me the right way, the way his kisses seem to fill my whole body.

Sometimes I can't get enough.

I finish showering and dress in a brand new hot pink bikini, running shorts and a white T-shirt. I toss a few things into my drawstring backpack, tuck my phone into my pocket and head down to the lobby just five minutes late.

Doan's waiting for me in a chair by a large set of bay windows.

"Morning, lovely," he says, getting to his feet when he sees me walking up to him. He bends down to kiss me lightly on the lips but I grab the back of his head for a deeper kiss.

When we break apart and our eyelids flutter open, he's looking at me with a lazy grin on his face.

"Well, hello to you, too," he says, and I smile and look away. "Ready to snorkel?"

"I can't wait! I've always wanted to do this."

He reaches down and laces his fingers through mine. "Me, too."

Our hotel is backed up right onto the beach so we walk out onto a wooden boardwalk that leads us over onto the sand, and to the shack where we'd been told we could get everything we'll need to start snorkeling.

We're the only ones waiting so the instructor has no trouble getting us set up. We each get a mask, a tube and fins. He walks us through securing the mask to our face, how to clear it if it fogs and how to breathe through the tube.

We strap the fins to our feet and awkwardly wade into the shallow water to practice breathing underwater. After a few minutes of standing about waist-deep in the chilly ocean and trying to float and get used to the water filling the snorkel, the instructor asks us if we think we've got it.

"I'm ready," I tell him, but when I look over at Doan, I'm shocked to realize he looks a lot more nervous than I feel. "Hey, you okay?"

He glances back at me and tries to smile but it comes out more like a grimace. "Yeah, yeah," he says. "No problem."

"Are you sure?"

He nods, and I look over at the instructor who's staring back at us with raised eyebrows.

"Everything cool?" he asks.

With one last look at Doan, I smile at the instructor and nod. "Yep. I think we got it."

"Great," he tells us. "Remember you left your IDs with me so don't leave the beach without returning your equipment this afternoon."

He walks out of the water and back up the sand to the snorkel shack, leaving Doan and me alone in the ocean.

"Ready?" I ask him.

I'm not prepared for what happens next.

"I can't do this," he says.

"What?"

He shakes his head and rubs his bare arms with his hands. "I don't like it. I can't."

I clumsily walk over to him through the water but it's a struggle in the flippers. "Why not?"

"I don't know. I just -- I panicked with that mask on over my face and the water coming into the tube and I can't."

"Yeah, you can," I say. "You heard Peter. It's normal to get some water in there. You got it out, right? You didn't breathe it in?"

He nods. "Yeah, I got it out."

"See?" I tell him, reaching out and gently stroking his arm. "And it's not like we even have to go all the way under the water or even that far from shore. Try it. We can stop whenever you want."

I'm trying to keep my voice soothing but on the inside, I'm all jumbled up. Part of me wants to scream at him that for someone who likes to race his car down busy streets, snorkeling should be no big deal. The other part is sort of weirdly attracted to whatever sensitive side of himself he's showing me right now.

It's kind of nice, I guess, knowing that Doan isn't all toughness and bravado all the time.

"I don't know."

"Did I ever tell you how scared I was to play baseball again?" I say. "Because I was. But I did it anyway. And that's kind of the thing about trying new things. What's the worst that can happen? You do something you've never done before and you hate it. So you're back right where you started, you know? But maybe you'll love it. Maybe it'll be worth it. But if you don't do it, you won't know."

I try to ignore the nagging feeling that I'm not taking my own advice with my music.

But it's getting harder.

He shakes his head and smiles at me. "You're something else, you know that?"

I grin and nod. "Oh, I know," I tell him, raising my eyebrows. "It's about time you figured it out."

Doan laughs. "You really want to do this, don't you?"

"Yeah. And I want to do it with you."

He lets out a small sigh. "Good enough for me. Let's do it."

He reaches out and takes my hand and we start toward the deeper waters. Eventually, when we can't touch the bottom of the ocean anymore, we start to swim.

"I'm gonna do it," I call over to him, and a minute later, I'm under the water, kicking down, and open my eyes.

I immediately look for him and see that he's stuck his face under the water but hasn't come all the way down with me.

I point to the green and yellow coral on the bottom of the ocean floor. Small gray fish swim near the plants, but I don't see any brightly-colored schools of fish yet.

I spend a few minutes under the water before kicking my way back to the surface. I take Doan's hand and we come up for air and lift our masks.

"What do you think?" I ask him.

He nods. "It's not so bad."

"Keep going?"

"Yeah."

I stick closer to the surface this time, keeping my hand in his, and we propel our way across the water, pointing things out to each other as we see them.

We've been in the ocean for what feels like an hour and haven't seen anything exciting. Fish, sure, but mostly small, bland-looking ones, and no brightly-colored coral. I'm not sure what I expected to find off the coast of Laguna Beach, but this isn't it.

"Want to head back?" I ask him as we take a break above the water.

Doan looks around at the mostly-empty water; just a few other small groups of snorkelers are around us. "I didn't realize how far out we came," he says. "Maybe we should. Let's keep snorkeling back, though."

I try to hide my smile at his suggestion. "Sure."

We duck back below the surface and swim toward the shore. And that's when I feel Doan's grip tighten on my hand. I look over at him and see he's pointing at something right below us.

I glance down and it's all I can do not to gasp.

Because now snorkeling is worth it.

I can't believe it.

Right here, right underneath me, floating along the ocean floor, is a giant sea turtle.

My eyes widen and I want to gasp but I can't with the mask covering my face. We stop swimming but Doan doesn't let go of my hand.

Neither of us moves as we watch the turtle lazily pilot itself near the ocean floor, and it's like I'm barely breathing.

Which is weird because I'm just looking at a turtle.

I've seen them countless times at the zoo before. Heck, I've even caught one or two wandering through our yard.

But they've never been so...big.

Or beautiful.

It's just a turtle, but I've never seen anything like this, the way it just effortlessly glides through the calm, cool, crisp water, how its arms flap and propel it forward, the way just one of its back legs grazes the sandy ocean floor with each movement.

And the whole time, I just like feeling Doan's hand in mine.

We watch the turtle, the brown spots decorating its head and shell as it swims farther away from us until it disappears into the dark corners of the ocean.

I look over at Doan, and point to the surface, and he nods. We swim back until our feet finally brush against the sandy bottom and we stand, lifting our masks from our faces.

Neither of us had gone back under the water after the seeing the turtle.

I want that to be my last memory -- my only memory, really -- of snorkeling in California.

Doan and I drag ourselves out of the water and onto the sandy shore. He grabs my hand and swings me over to him.

"Thanks," he tells me, pulling my wet body against his. "That was incredible."

I can't keep the smile from spreading across my face. "You're welcome."

He leans down, one of his arms wrapped around my waist, and kisses me right here in the middle of the beach.

"The perfect morning," he says when he break apart. He looks down at me with a grin. "Now let's go play some ball."

***

We're on the field against a team from a suburb outside of Los Angeles. Doan's back on the mound, and the Scorpions are riding a 2-0 lead in the bottom of the sixth inning. I'm confident we'll win as long as he's the one pitching.

And he's got a no-hitter going and I'm holding my breath with every wind-up of his arm, hoping this isn't going to be the batter that breaks his streak.

I haven't done much in the game so far. I walked both times I got up to bat, but haven't managed to cross home plate yet.

Except none of that matters right now because of how well Doan's playing.

Now he's in a bit of a tough spot, and I'm not sure how he's going to work his way out of this one. He's walked the bases loaded. There are two outs with the sixth hitter of the inning on his way to the plate.

But all it takes is an out, and it has to be this one.

The batter stares in at Doan, and I find myself staring hard at the batter. Like I think I can psych him out from third base or something.

It's only weird if it doesn't work, right?

The first pitch flies in across the plate. Strike one. I suck in some air. Just two more now.

Doan readies himself for the next one, then lets it go.

It sails in on the batter who swings and misses as the ball lands safely in the catcher's glove with a thud.

Two down now.

I want to squeeze my eyes shut as the third pitch comes but I force myself to watch.

The batter swings at the pitch again, this time making contact, and the ball flies out to the left fielder. He gives it chase and it lands harmlessly in his glove.

Phew.

Relief for Doan floods through me, and he points at the left fielder before jogging off the mound and into the dugout.

I'm not one of the three hitters due up first in the top of the inning so I take my seat along the bench.

Doan drops down next to me. "Hey," he says, lifting his cap from his head and wiping at his sweaty brow with his arm. The charcoal under his eyes has already started to smudge in the heat.

"Nice out."

He nods. "Tough inning."

"Yeah, but you can handle it." I'm about to say something else about his no-hitter when he holds up a hand to stop me.

"No!" he exclaims, sticking his fingers in his ears and closing his eyes. "Don't even say it."

I wait for him to cautiously blink them open, then unclog his ears. "Say what?" I reply with a grin.

He stares at me for a second, then smiles. "Thanks."

"I didn't peg you as the superstitious type," I tell him, fidgeting with a loose thread hanging off the side of my glove.

He shrugs. "I'm not with most things."

"But you are with this."

"What gave it away?"

I just laugh and he smiles, and we sit here like this, neither of us saying anything, watching baseball.

It doesn't take long for the other team's pitcher to retire our batters in order and we're trotting back out onto the field for the final inning of the game.

Doan's still on the mound, hoping to close out his no-hitter.

And my stomach is all tangled up in hundreds of tiny, tight knots.

The first batter takes two practice swings at the plate before he squares up. He stares in at Doan, a look of fierce determination in his eyes, and I kind of want to wipe the smirk right off his face.

But Doan handles him perfectly. He pops up the first pitch he sees, straight back, and the catcher grabs it safely behind home plate.

One gone.

The next batter is just as easy of an out as he grounds to shortstop.

No sweat.

I'm watching Doan the whole time as he deals his fourth pitch of the inning to the third, and hopefully last, batter.

And I'm still watching Doan as the batter hits the ball and it rolls right to me. I snap to attention and manage to scoop it up and fire it to first base. It's gonna be close; I want to squeeze my eyes shut as the ball flies through the air to the baseman's open glove.

How could I have been so stupid? How could I have not been paying attention to the batter? Why is it so easy for Doan to distract me like this? Why -- ?

"YES!"

I'm interrupted from my swarming stream of self-pity by Doan's triumphant shout as the team flies in around him on the mound.

My eyes widen; the ball must've made it to first base on time.

I haven't ruined it for him.

And he's just thrown a no-hitter.

I run in toward the mound and wiggle my way through the bodies until I find him.

He beams at me and pulls me hard against him. He leans down and kisses me, and I wrap my arms around his neck, and the next thing I know, we're *both* being lifted into the air by our teammates. Doan, because he's tossed a no-hitter, and me, because I'm attached to Doan.

We break apart, look at each other and laugh, and he grabs my hand.

I let go and slip down off of Dave's shoulders.

This is Doan's moment, another page of his book, one that I'm happy to be on, but it isn't about me.

And mostly I just want him to have a story that he's finally happy to share.

***

Dad and I are walking on the beach later that night after the win. Doan had wanted to go for a late swim but when Dad cornered me as I was on my way to meet him at the pool, I couldn't say no.

We're not talking much as we walk, but I'm enjoying the feeling of the wet sand between my toes as I carry my flip-flops in one hand.

"It's beautiful here, isn't it?" Dad finally asks, and I wonder if he's about to get to the point now, or if there even is a point to this walk at all.

"Yeah, it's nice."

"Your mom and I used to bring you and Justin here when you were kids," he tells me, and I swallow hard, already feeling my mouth start to run a little dry. "Do you remember that?"

I shake my head and don't look at him. "Nope. It feels like my first trip to California."

"That's too bad," he says. "We always had a great time, the four of us. I loved being with you guys."

Now I swing my head in his direction. "What are you talking about?"

Dad looks at me. "We never really talked about what happened, did we?"

"Dad, I don't want -- "

"Wait," he says, holding up his hand. "Let me, okay, Holly? We don't have to bring it up ever again but let me say this."

I let out a quiet sigh. "Okay."

"I didn't know that I'd ever get a chance to tell you all the things I've wanted to," Dad says as we walk along, neither of us looking at the other. "But when you moved back, I decided it was time. You're old enough now. Holly, you know I never meant to ruin our family."

I open my mouth to respond, to spare him this, but he stops me.

"Wait," he says. "Please. I never meant to do that. I know that I did and I knew that I would, but I suppose on some levels, it was something that had to happen. Your mother and I weren't happy anymore. It's always hard when something comes to an end, even when it's broken, but sometimes there's relief there, too. And the truth is, she and I both knew that, one day, this would be for the best. And that's happened."

He takes a deep breath before continuing. "Your mom's happier now than she had been with me for the last couple years we were together. Tanya and I are having a baby. Justin is great and I'm so proud of you," he says. "I don't want to trivialize it and say that everything worked out for the best, but it did. We might not have ended up where we thought we'd be, but I think we ended up where we're supposed to be."

I'm letting all of Dad's words sink into my head as he says them. I know that I'm not supposed to be okay with this, that I'm supposed to be angry and sulking and not letting him off the hook, and maybe fight, cry, scream, but I don't feel any of those things.

I was mad at him when I got to Arizona. I didn't want to be here, and I definitely didn't want to be living with him. But after two months in the desert, it's all fading away. I know my mom is happy, and I know Dad is, too. He's right when he says Justin's good, and I don't know what, exactly, there is to be proud of me for, but I'm not unhappy, either.

I'm okay with where I am and I'm okay with where I've been. None of those things would have happened if Dad hadn't cheated.

I wish I could have grown up in a house with two parents who were in love and happy and had the white picket fence and the dog and the station wagon and all those things you're supposed to want, but I didn't, and that's okay, too.

I'm figuring it out, anyway.

For the first time in what seems like forever, it finally feels like everything is falling into place. I'm home. I have my brother. I have my parents, even if they don't have each other. And there's Doan and Natalie and baseball, and what more do I need?

I look over at Dad as all these thoughts run through my head, and he's staring back at me, and I'm certain I see fear in his eyes that I'm about to snap and yell and tell him all the reasons that he's a terrible father.

"It's okay," I say instead. I don't know what else to tell him. "I mean that."

He frowns. "Are you sure?"

"Dad, I'm sure," I say, my voice stronger than I remember hearing it in a long time. "It's over. It happened already. And like you said, it's worked out okay. We're all okay."

He nods and takes a few shaky steps toward me and folds me into his arms and I hug him back, tightly, and it's the first time in a long time that a hug from Dad doesn't feel wrong.

And I can't help but think back to the night that Doan came upstairs and heard my singing and told me that Dad was planning on asking me to join his baseball team.

I remember the horror I felt, the dread, the cold sweat that washed over me at the idea of spending that much time with him.

And I remember what Doan told me, that there's never enough time with family. That there's always a way to forgive your family.

I just don't remember thinking that he was right.

***

"We had a good talk," I tell Doan when I find him out by the hotel pool after Dad and I get back from the beach.

He beams at me from the water. I'm dangling my legs in the pool as I sit along the edge. "I'm really happy for you, Holls."

I realize that I'm happy for me, too. I still don't know if Dad and I needed to have that conversation, but I know it helped him, so I'm glad it happened.

"You know what else?" I say, the idea that's been rattling around in the back of my head for the last hour about to come to the surface. "I kind of think I want to try singing again. In front of people. Well, at least as many people as you'll see at Gemma's, anyway."

Doan's grin gets even wider. "Are you serious?"

I nod and bite my lip. "Yeah, I think so."

And it sounds right even when I hear it out loud. Dad telling me that he's so happy with how everyone is doing lately got me thinking. Mom's where she wants to be, and so is he, and I'm pretty sure Justin's good, too.

Walking back up to the hotel, I'd realized that only one thing is really missing from what I want to be doing.

And that's sharing my music.

So I'm going to do it.

"Why?" Doan asks. "I know you wanted to before, but you were so pissed to see me there."

I shrug. "It feels right. It's time to do it for real."

"Will you come?" I ask him. "To the show?"

He shakes his head and smiles. "You really have to ask?"

"Just want to make sure."

"Come on," he says. "I was at your first show, too, remember? And I didn't even get to see you play. Pretty sure you owe me one now."

I laugh and think back to how it feels like that happened so long ago but it was really just a month.

"I know," he says, studying my face. "Feels like forever ago, right?" He's absently stroking the skin on my leg with his thumb.

"Yeah, it really does."

I smile and lean down to kiss him and feel his soft, sweet lips against mine, gentle at first, but there's more urgency as I run my fingers through his hair.

He wraps his arms around my waist and pulls me toward him and we tumble down into the water, hitting it with a splash.

We're both laughing when he come up for air.

"Forgot where I was there," he says with a chuckle.

I put my arms and legs around him, and hold on as he swims us lazily through the pool.

"It's perfect here," I tell him. "Right now, like this."

He looks at me and nods. "I wouldn't want to be anywhere else. Or with anyone else."

I try to keep the smile from taking over my face, but it's hard when I'm looking right at him, and he's so lovely and wonderful and gorgeous and, well, mine.

Having Doan here with me is enough to make me feel like the luckiest girl in the world.

Like I'm where I've always belonged.

CHAPTER SEVENTEEN

I sit in the front seat of my comfortable, familiar Honda, a slight wave of nausea bubbling up in my stomach as I try to steady myself to do something I'm not sure I'm ready for but that I know I want.

I suck in a deep breath and hop out of my car. I pull my guitar and song notebook out of the backseat and walk steadily toward Gemma's. I'm nervous, but it feels different this time. I don't have the same sense of dread. I want to be here. I need to do this.

And mostly I'm just glad Doan will be here later to support me when I need him.

Natalie is standing behind the counter when I walk in.

"Hey!" she exclaims. "You came!"

"'Course I did. I'm on the list."

She shrugs. "Doesn't mean much, does it? Let's see if we can actually get you on stage tonight."

I smile. "I promise this time."

"Hey, I want you to meet Shane," she says as a tall guy with longer, wavy blonde hair and a solid athlete's body comes walking out of the back room. "He's home from summer training in Europe. Shane, this is Holly."

"Good to finally meet you," he says, holding out a hand to me before Natalie nestles herself under the crook of his shoulder and smiles at him.

It's obvious when watching the two of them together that they're in love. That they're right. There's no mistaking the way she looks at him, or the protective arm he wraps around her.

Just a few weeks ago, I'm pretty sure this would've made me insane with envy even if I wouldn't admit it.

But now...

"Nice to meet you too," I say. "I've heard lots about you and hockey."

Shane grins and smiles at his girlfriend. "Why am I not surprised?" He points to the guitar resting on the floor next to my feet. "You playing tonight?"

"Yeah. Definitely."

"Is Doan coming?" Natalie asks, raising her eyebrows suggestively at me.

I try not to blush but I'm pretty sure it doesn't work. "He's supposed to be here, yeah."

She claps her hands together and gives a little squeal, and Shane smiles and shakes his head before leaning down and brushing a quick kiss against her hair.

"Yes!" she exclaims. "I knew it!"

"I don't even know what we're doing," I tell her.

"I do," she replies. "The look on your face says it all."

I blush again. "I'm gonna put this in the back and get to work. The napkins are looking low."

Natalie shoots me a knowing, triumphant smile as I walk to the back and take a second for myself in the back.

I set my guitar and notebook down along the wall and wrap an apron around my waist.

I look at the guitar resting peacefully and smile.

It's finally going to happen.

Open mic night starts in twenty minutes but I'm not scheduled to play until nine. Doan said he'd come early to hang out and I can't wait to see him. We'd mostly just slept the entire bus ride back to Arizona on Sunday night, and I haven't seen him since.

I push my way back through the swinging door with extra napkins and straws tucked under my arms and walk over to the counter where we keep those goods.

Shane's sitting at a table near the door sipping from a mug and reading a book, while Natalie puts fresh cakes in the glass pastry display. I watch them as I absently fill the napkin dispensers. Every now and then, he glances up from his reading to look at her and smile, and every time he puts his head back down, she happens to look at him and gets the same happy, faraway look on her face.

And that just makes me smile and look to the door, waiting for Doan to walk in for me.

I turn my back so I can stock up on straws when the bells jingle and I feel a tap on my shoulder.

Already smiling, I whirl around, ready to fling my arms around Doan and wrap him up in a giant hug when I have to immediately throw on the brakes.

"Whoa," I say as I hold out my hand against this guy's chest to steady myself. "Uh, sorry."

He raises an eyebrow, then looks down at my hand pressed against him, and I quickly pull it away.

"You're here to sing, right?" I ask, recognizing him now that I have a chance to look at him as the heat in my cheeks fades. He came up to me before the last open mic night, too, to ask about setting up his equipment.

But I hope he doesn't remember me.

Or at least what we talked about that day.

He nods. "Yep. You too?"

I smile. "Yeah."

"How'd it go last time? You were so nervous."

I fiddle with the straw in my hands. "Uh, yeah. It didn't really -- tonight'll be my first time playing here."

Adam -- I have to glance down at Natalie's notebook to make sure that's his name -- raises an eyebrow. "What happened?"

I shake my head. "Too much to explain now," I say with a wry smile. "But it worked out. It's okay now."

"Good. Everyone should always feel good playing their stuff."

"Yeah. I'm excited about it." I look back at the notebook resting on the counter. "You guys are up first again. Set up whenever you're ready."

"Thanks," he says. "Maybe I'll stick around to see you play, too."

I smile. "Good luck," I tell him before turning around and returning my attention to the straws.

I close my eyes for a second and suck in a deep breath.

There's no going back now.

And that's exactly the way I want it.

Doan isn't here.

We're six sets in now and it's almost 9:30.

There are just two people left and then it's my turn to play.

I've called him three times. I've sent him text messages.

I can't take my eyes off the door.

And there's nothing I can do about the endless, relentless churning in my stomach.

I'm pretty sure I'm going to throw up.

Telling myself to stay calm, he'll be here, you know he'll come, does nothing for me.

Because he isn't coming.

I know it.

Natalie's giving me sad looks from the table she's sharing with Shane, but I can barely stand to look at them.

It's like staring at a picture that only shows you what you want but will never have.

And I just really don't understand how he could do this to me.

How I'm supposed to get up on that stage and play without him here.

I need him.

And then Natalie's standing by my side.

"I'm sorry, Holly," she says. "But he could still come, you know."

I shake my head, swallowing hard, trying to keep the fast-growing lump in my throat from getting even more out of control. "He won't."

She sets her mouth in a thin, grim line. "I'm sure he has a good reason, though."

"He doesn't need a good reason. It's just who he is."

"What?"

I shake my head and press my fingers hard against my eyes, like that'll help me cram the tears threatening to spill over back in. "I've known it since the moment I met him. This is my fault. I let him fool me."

"No, you didn't. He's a good guy. I've known him a lot longer than you," she says. "If he promised he'd be here, and he isn't, then he's got to have an explanation."

"Everyone always says that," I say. "'Oh, I'm sure there's a good explanation.' Well, that's just great. But an explanation doesn't make it okay. An explanation doesn't make me hurt any less right now. An explanation doesn't mean he can't sent a two-word text letting me know what's up."

"Holly."

I turn to face her. "What? You aren't exactly saying anything that's making me feel better here."

"I'm sorry," she says again. "I just don't want you to jump to conclusions. Don't be upset if you don't have to be."

It's all I can do not to roll my eyes and laugh. "He promised me he would be here, Natalie, and he isn't. That's all I know right now. And I think that's a pretty good reason to be upset."

The person on Natalie's list in front of me takes the stage. I glance down at my phone one more time even though I know it's pointless.

I'm right. There's nothing on the screen.

Natalie doesn't say anything as I sulk through this guy's set, not taking my eyes off the door the whole time.

"Please tell me you're still going to play," she says without looking at me.

I swallow again and now I know I've lost the battle with my tears as they slowly slide from my eyes.

"That's all you care about? Your open mic night?" I snap, pressing furiously at my eyes, trying to jam the tears back inside.

"Holly, come on. You know that isn't true. I just want you to do this, okay? For once. And for you."

The guy strums the last chord on his guitar, thanks the handful of people who shower him with a smattering round of applause, grabs his notebook and walks off the stage.

All of a sudden, I feel like the spotlight that doesn't even exist is beating right down on me, hot and unrelenting, and beads of sweat pop up along my hairline.

"Holly?" Natalie says.

I look down at my phone one more time.

Nothing.

Just like I knew there would be.

I look over at the door one more time.

No one.

Just like I knew there would be.

My eyes wander back to the now-empty stage that's waiting for me. The stool with my name on it. The microphone waiting for my words. The music stand that wants to hold my songs.

I want to do this.

But he isn't here.

And for some reason, I can't.

I need him for this, and I wish I don't. But he promised me.

The sobs come first. They bubble up in my throat and spill out with every heave of my shoulders.

The tears pour from my eyes. I do nothing to try to stop them. I can't breathe and I can't think and I definitely can't play the guitar. I run to the back, pushing my way through the swinging employee's only door to safety, where I don't have to see the stage and feel it calling out to me.

I lean back up against the wall, right next to my guitar, and sink to the ground. Natalie's shaky voice fills the cafe as she thanks everyone for coming out and reminds us we'll be back here again next week, same time, same place.

Fantastic.

My song notebook falls off the top of the guitar case when I bump into it and spills open to the last page, the page with the song I could never quite finish scribbled onto it.

I snatch a pen off the desk and start writing.

"When you said you'd be there
I thought I could believe in you
When you said you cared
I thought I could believe in you

I've been down this road before

And I didn't think you'd bring me back

But now I'm here again

And I'm afraid I'll never get away

Now you're gone

And I know you aren't coming back

They say it's darkest before dawn

But my heart's already cracked

I should've known, should've known should've
known

What I didn't know, didn't know, didn't know

But how do you know what you won't let yourself
see?

And now I'm scared I'll never be free."

I don't even know that I'm still crying until I look up from the page and see tear splatters smearing the ink.

But I don't care. It's finished.

The song that's haunted me for years is finally finished.

It starts in Pennsylvania and ends in Arizona.

But realizing that shows me how little has really changed for me. Nothing is different at all.

And maybe that scars my heart the deepest tonight.

Because it isn't the ending I'm looking for.

CHAPTER EIGHTEEN

Natalie sends me home without asking me to stay behind and help clean up as part of the end of my shift, and for the first time, I hadn't felt much like arguing with her.

I'm not sure if it's Doan standing me up or finally writing that song, but I'm exhausted when I collapse on top of my bed in my pajamas about an hour later.

I kept my phone off the whole ride home.

Part of me doesn't want to keep checking to see if Doan finally called, because that same part really wants him to have a good reason for not showing up tonight.

I want to believe that there are missed calls from him on my phone, voicemails and text messages. I want to -- and maybe I need to -- believe that he still cares about me. That he ever cared about me.

And then the other part is just terrified that he hasn't reached out at all and I don't want to deal with the inevitable gut punch that'll come from seeing nothing from him on the screen.

But I can't keep my phone off forever and I've got some morbid curiosity, so I reach into the pocket of my jeans, dig it out and turn it on. It takes a few minutes to power up and I turn it over and rest it on the bed next to me.

When it bleeps a minute later, my heart leaps up into my throat and I grab at it, ready for the smile to form across my face as I read his explanation and everything makes sense. I can practically taste the relief I'm going to feel.

But when I turn it over and see a text from Natalie waiting for me -- and nothing, absolutely nothing, from Doan -- I want to punt the phone off my balcony and into the plunging valley below us.

Dammit.

But with a sigh, I open Natalie's message.

Just want to make sure you got home okay :)

I want to type back in all caps and tell her that her checking in on me has only made me feel more miserable, but I know she means well. I type out something quick and boring and useless to let her know I'm home and thanks for asking, and send it back, hoping she gets the hint not to send me another message and get my hopes up again.

I'm not sure I can take that.

I put the phone on silent and place it on the pillow next to my head and crawl underneath the covers, sure that I won't get any sleep tonight.

All I can see is Doan, Doan, Doan. It's like I'm watching the movie of us with no power button.

There he is, grinning at me, his tan, strong arms dangerously alluring as he teases me about speeding down the road on my first day in town.

And again when I spin over in my pool chair and find him spraying me down with sunscreen like some kind of weirdo. I'll never forget that tangle of emotions I felt seeing him again at my dad's house; the confusing appeal of realizing that I loved knowing he wasn't totally lost to me, that he wasn't going to be nothing more than a meaningless encounter one summer afternoon.

There's pepperoni pizzas and baseball practice and batting cages and mini golf.

Mini golf.

The first night I ever really felt like I could be myself around him. The appeal, the attraction, had been there all along, that much I can admit. But that was the very first time I ever let myself consider that maybe something could be there with us, and even then, I remember being skeptical.

But I was right.

It was.

Even if only for me.

There's coaching and turtles and oceans and pools and water gun fights and promises that hadn't fallen on deaf ears, but had been made by false tongues.

And then there's that first night he came to Gemma's, when I'd been set to play my music without any help from anyone.

He'd been so eager, so optimistic, so -- I don't know. But he wanted us to be friends.

And I believed him.

I just wish I could know what happened now.

Because not knowing if my heart is supposed to be broken might be worse than having a broken heart at all.

His words and his smile and that damn twinkle in his eye keep floating in front of my closed eyes and I'm sure I'm no closer to sleep than I was after my fourth coffee of the day.

With a nervous pit in my stomach, I give in and peek at my phone screen one last time.

Still blank.

And the crack in my heart gets a little bit deeper.

Because honestly?

I'm not sure I can come up with a single good reason for what he's doing.

And if I can't justify his behavior, then how can I let myself keep falling for him, even if I want to forget this whole thing ever happened?

It's a question I don't have any answers to.

But I really wish I did.

CHAPTER NINETEEN

I wake up in a pile of used tissues with my eyes practically sealed shut from the dried up tears I couldn't get to stop coming last night.

Eventually, I'd fallen asleep, still crying, but I have no idea when and no idea how.

And I'm pretty sure my dreams were even crueler than reality.

In them, I'd had the chance to perform at Gemma's, the chance to play the songs I wanted to sing to people for the first time.

And Doan had been there, in the same seat he'd taken when he came to the cafe uninvited for the first open mic night.

Each time I'd looked out into the audience, I saw him smiling back at me, nodding, tapping his foot to the beat.

And whenever I saw him, it only made me want to keep going, to keep singing.

But now I guess I'll never know what that's like.

I look at my phone, and while there's still nothing from Doan or anyone else, a calendar alert pops up reminding me that we have a baseball game today.

My heart drops.

Baseball.

And Doan.

I'd known that I'd see him there, of course, but it hadn't exactly been something I'd given a lot of thought to, and I definitely hadn't remembered that we have a game this morning.

I glance at the clock and realize that I need to be at the field in half an hour. For a second, I consider staying in bed and wallowing, but then I think of Justin and Dad and my other teammates, and how we all really do want a shot at the postseason tournament and silly pig trophy even if they don't mean all that much, and I know I'm not going to let them down by not showing up.

So I drag myself into the shower, dig out my baseball uniform, find my bat and glove, and force myself into my car.

I think of nothing but Doan the whole way to the field.

I'm not sure what he's going to say to me, but I know now that I won't breathe a word to him.

This is his decision. He's doing this.

If he didn't show up last night because he wants nothing to do with me, then I'm not going to go crying to him about it. I'll let him have what he wants, which is none of me.

And if he didn't come because he's got some great reason I can't think of, then he should be sprinting over to me first thing to throw himself at my feet and beg for my forgiveness.

Or something like that, anyway.

But this is all on him.

He did this to us, and if he wants to fix it, he knows exactly where to find me.

I pull the car up alongside the diamond and notice that Doan's pick-up truck isn't in the parking lot. I'd promised myself I wouldn't look for it, but who are we kidding?

I'm a freakin' mess.

Justin and Dad are both in the dugout and greet me cheerfully. I'm pretty sure my brother has no idea what happened, and I hope my eyes aren't as red and gross as they were an hour ago.

"How was work last night?" Justin asks.

"Oh," I say, trying to keep my voice light and airy. "It was good. What'd you do?"

"Doan and I shot some pool and grabbed a couple pitchers of beer," he says with a shrug, and it's obvious to me that he has no idea how much his words sting me. It's like a thousand wasps all decided right now is a great time to attack, and they're all going after my heart.

I drop down onto the bench and try hard not to seem rattled, but I'm pretty sure my breathing's funny and my head feels like it's about to blast off into outer space.

I mean, what?

Beers? And pool?

That's what kept Doan from coming to Gemma's last night?

There's no emergency. No one's dead or in the hospital. No car accident. He hasn't broken an arm and probably didn't even lose his phone.

All of those things, of course, had passed through my mind on a loop as possible explanations for why he didn't come.

But no.

Beers. And pool.

With my brother.

Is he *kidding*?

Suddenly, I'm not so much sad as I am downright livid. How dare he do this to me? How dare he play me like this? How could he possibly --

"Hey, guys."

I freeze, right in the middle of my mental assassination of Doan Riley.

Because none other than the victim himself has just strolled into the dugout like he doesn't have a care in the world, tossed his bag aside and greeting the rest of us all casual and cool.

Like his insides aren't being slowly ripped out the same way mine are.

And I'm just sitting here wondering if this is really my life.

I immediately start rooting around in my bag, refusing to look at him, anger definitely still coursing strong through me.

Beer and pool.

I shake my head, trying to keep a bitter laugh from creeping out.

And then something happens.

I'm not sure why, exactly, I feel compelled to look up at Doan Riley at this exact moment, but I do, and my eyes meet his, and there's a stunning sadness behind them that disappears right away, but I saw it, and it's not what I expect.

So for the millionth time in what feels like five minutes, I'm confused all over again.

I wait just a second for him to approach me, but he doesn't, and he breaks our eye contact a few beats later.

I start to feel myself getting closer and closer to snapping when Dad stands up and calls the team to a huddle around him. I make sure to stand as far away from Doan as possible; I can't even see him from where I am, and that's a good thing.

Dad gives us a pep talk that I don't hear, then sends us off into the field to start the game.

As I reach for my glove to take my place at third base, Dad reaches out and stops me.

"Hey," he says. "Wait. Holly. Are you okay? You seem distracted."

I shake my head. "No, I'm good."

"Are you sure?" he asks. "You can DH today if you need to."

"No way," I tell him, knowing that means I'll just sit on the bench and wallow in my own miserable, angry thoughts. "I'm fine. I just want to play baseball."

I'm pretty sure my cheeks try to smile for the first time in the last 24 hours when I realize how true it is.

This baseball diamond, even if it means Doan's right under my nose, is the only place I want to be to get through this.

I need the game.

So I do what I know best and jog out onto the field and over to third base.

Doan pitched in our last game in California so he isn't on the mound, and for some reason, he isn't in the bullpen, either. He's hanging out in the dugout with a couple other guys.

But I'm determined now to only focus on the game.

It's why I'm here.

And I refuse to let my eyes wander over to him, to see if he's looking at me first.

He won't be.

Right?

He is.

I break my own promise when I look at him, but quickly glance away when our eyes meet again.

What is with him?

He's making me nuts. I can't take much more of this. I'm not going to be able to play baseball if this is how it's going to be.

We're going to have to talk about this, one way or another, because not knowing is going to make me crazy.

And just like that, the top half of the first inning is over, and I realize I haven't seen a single pitch.

That, you might be able to guess, isn't a great thing when you're on the field.

Oops.

I wander back into the dugout. I don't bat until sixth, so there's a reasonable chance that I won't be up at all in the bottom of the first.

I'm not sure what comes over me, but the next thing I know, I'm throwing my glove to the bench and marching right over to Doan Riley.

"Let's talk," I say, interrupting his conversation with another pitcher.

Ben looks at me with raised eyebrows before shrugging and getting up off the bench.

Doan doesn't meet my eye.

"Well?" I say at last.

He finally looks at me. "Holls, I don't think I can."

"Don't," I say through gritted teeth, "call me Holls."

"I -- I don't know what to say," he says.

"Come with me. We're not talking here."

I ignore the fact that he's just said he doesn't want to talk to me, turn and walk out of the dugout and head over to the fence near the parking lot.

I'm pretty sure I'm mad enough to make a scene if he doesn't follow me.

And he might realize that, too, because when I turn around, he's right behind me.

"Well?" I demand for the second time.

He lets out a sigh. "I don't know what you want me to say, Holly."

I lift my eyebrows. "You've gotta be kidding me."

"Okay," he says. "Fair. I know what you want me to say. Look, for whatever it's worth, I'm sorry I wasn't there last night. But I couldn't be."

"Why?"

He lets out a sigh and shakes his head. "It's so damn complicated."

"Beers and pool with my brother is complicated?"

"I'm sorry," he says. "Look, if you want to talk about this, it isn't going to be here. Come with me after the game."

"We're talking about this now, Doan, or not at all and this is the end. Your choice."

"We're in the middle of a game, Holly."

"I don't give a damn about the game."

Doan looks back over at the field, then down at me. He sighs, then motions me to follow him. We walk over to his truck and I get into the passenger seat.

He pulls his phone out of the console, shoots off a text to my brother to tell him not to expect us back for the rest of the game, then squeals out of the parking lot without a word to me.

"Well?" I demand.

The irony of leaving in the middle of a game isn't lost on me when the only reason I'm here in the first place is so I don't let my teammates down.

He shakes his head. "Wait, okay? Just wait. We'll talk when we get there."

"Where are we going?"

"Holly, *please*!" he says, and I'm not sure he's ever taken this pleading but also scarily harsh tone with me.

I do as he says and flop back against my seat in silence, arms crossed over my chest.

Doan accelerates down the road, and I watch as the speedometer creeps higher and higher. I weigh my irritation with him for asking me to be quiet with the growing beads of sweat popping up on my hands.

"Hey," I finally say. "Maybe slow down?"

He doesn't look at me. "I know how to drive."

I suck in a breath. "You sure about that? You do remember how we met, right?"

He throws up his hands in the air and slams them back down on the wheel. "Have you ever let me forget? Just once? Have you ever let me forget?"

"Maybe I don't think you deserve to forget!" I yell back. "Maybe you're exactly who I thought you were this whole damn time, Doan."

"Or maybe you have no idea what you're talking about."

My eyes flash as I turn in my seat to face him. "That," I hiss in a low growl, "is because you never tell me anything about you."

The engine's roaring louder than I've ever heard a car engine before. It's almost like it's screaming beneath all the stress Doan's putting it under.

"Doan," I say, my voice calmer than before. "I really think you should -- "

I'm still looking at him when I see his eyes grow wide and his mouth drop open but no sounds comes out.

And I'm still looking at him when the sickening crunch of metal colliding with metal streams into my ears, the overpowering smell of burning rubber fills my nose, and the darkness closes my eyes even though I'm positive they're still open.

I'm still looking at him when everything goes black, the world fades away and the only sound I hear is nothing.

***

I wake up what feels like minutes later and find myself staring at a white ceiling in a room with white walls and a faint, steady beeping humming away from somewhere behind me.

I blink a few times and try to sit up and then Dad's face is inches from mine and I almost scream.

"Jeez!" I exclaim, then I start coughing and can't stop.

Dad backs away, but he doesn't go very far. "Holly!" he cries, and there's a strange sense of relief in his voice, and I don't understand it. "Take it easy. Don't overexert yourself. Justin, get the nurse."

My brother scurries past the foot of the bed I just now realizing I'm lying in.

"Huh?" I say between sputtering coughs.

"You're okay," Dad breathes, and he finally backs away enough for me to feel like I can let out some air. "Thank goodness, thank goodness."

"Of course I'm okay," I choke out, but I have to admit, I'm a little worried about why talking suddenly seems so hard. "What the heck, Dad?"

He just shakes his head and presses his thumb and index finger into his eyes. A few seconds later, he looks at me.

"You were in an accident, Holly," he says. "In Doan's pick-up truck during the game. Do you remember?"

I raise an eyebrow and think back but the last thing I remember is demanding Doan follow me out of the dugout at the game.

"Nope," I say. "But I'm pretty sure there's no amnesia going on here. I remember everything leading up to whatever accident you're talking about."

Dad looks at me and laughs, but there isn't a lot of humor in the sound. "Okay," he says. "Well, I guess that's good. Your brother went to get the nurse. She should be here any minute."

"Doan's car?" I ask.

Dad nods, and I feel a pit form in my stomach. I still don't remember what happened but if it was bad enough to land me in the hospital and put *that* look in Dad's eyes...well, I'm not sure I want to know the details.

But I have to know if he's okay.

"He's -- ?"

"Fine. He's fine."

I look up and over and here he is, standing in the door leaning up against the frame like he used to do in my bedroom.

I can see a small scratch above his left eye but that's it. No bruises. No broken bones. No hospital bed. I look down at my own wrist in a cast and narrow my eyes.

"Glad to see it," I say, the panic about him being okay fleeing and being replaced by a flooding sense of irritability.

How the heck am I supposed to throw a baseball and play the guitar with my hand all wrapped up in this thing?

"Yeah, I don't care about me," Doan says, taking a step into the room. "How are you?"

"She's going to be okay," Dad answers for me. "Just a broken wrist. She's lucky."

I don't miss the anger in his voice, and I can't say I'm surprised.

But I don't really feel much of anything.

The nurse walks in and ushers Dad, Justin and Doan out. She takes my vitals and talks to me about my wrist and says I can go home in the morning because they just want to make sure I'm not concussed or anything like that overnight.

I'm not really listening. I want her to go away.

And I want Doan to come back.

But when the nurse leaves, it's just Dad and Justin who enter the room.

"Visiting hours are almost over," Dad tells me, and my eyes widen.

"Can you send Doan in? He didn't leave, did he?"

Dad looks agitated, but he just nods and Justin walks out into the hall and then Doan is in my room.

Dad and my brother make no move to go.

"Can we have a minute?" I ask them pointedly.

They look startled, but hurry out of the room, closing the door behind them.

And then it's just me and him.

"So," I say, sitting up in bed. "Hi."

"Holly, I'm so sorry."

"For what?" I ask.

He furrows his brow. "For the accident. For landing you in here. I never meant to hurt you. I was driving too fast but I was so confused, I didn't know what I was doing. You know how I am but it's not -- "

I hold up the broken wrist that I can't barely feel right now. "You think this is what hurt me?"

He stops, mid-sentence. "What?"

"You think I care about a stupid broken wrist? I mean, yeah, I'm gonna be pissed when I try to throw a baseball around, but God, Doan, if you think the accident is what you need to be apologizing for, then I really have no idea what I'm going to do with you."

He sits down carefully on the end of my hospital bed.

"Gemma's?" he finally asks.

"Ya think?" I shoot back.

"I'm sorry about that, too, Holly. I don't know why I did it but I just felt like -- I don't know. You were getting too close. I was getting too close. But it isn't your fault. I just freaked out."

"About what? I don't get it."

He throws his head back and rubs his face with his hands. "Dammit, Holly, you're not making this easy." He takes a deep breath. "I don't want this to go away. You and me, I mean."

I stare at him. "Then you should have been there for me when you promised you would be."

"Don't you think I know that?"

"Then why weren't you?" It's all I can do to keep from raising my voice but I don't want to attract the attention of the nurses.

"Because I don't let people get close to me. I can't do it."

"Yeah, yeah, I've heard that before," I say, waving my hand. "It's an excuse and it's a lame one. Everyone wants to be happy, Doan, but too many people are scared to give up what makes them comfortable to make that happen. You're never going to be happy if you don't risk what you have now to to get where you want to be."

"It's not that simple for me."

I try not to roll my eyes. "Everyone always thinks they're the exception to this," I say. "But guess what? Everyone's been hurt before and everyone's going to have to get over it and try again if being happy is what they really want. No one is an exception here."

"Holly, my brother *died* in a war zone," Doan says. "Don't you think that makes it a little harder for me to get close to people?"

All of me freezes except for my stomach, which plummets straight to my toes.

My mouth runs dry, I can't move, have I heard him right?

"Wh-what?" I stammer out.

"Why are you looking at me like that?" he asks, confusion clouding his eyes. "You know this."

"You never told me," I say. "I'd remember something like that."

"I just thought you heard," he says. "Everyone in town knows. I figured if Justin didn't tell you then Natalie definitely did."

"No one wanted me to tell me the things they all thought I should hear from you," I say, starting to piece together how all of this blew up.

He rubs his forehead. "But the things you said," he tells me, his voice growing softer. "You asked me if I miss him a lot. And all those things I told you about not having enough time with family. I just thought you knew what I was talking about."

"Doan, I had no idea. None. I thought he was overseas. Deployed. Coming home soon."

He shakes his head. "He'd still have his dog tags," he says quietly, and I watch as his fingers absently go to the chain hanging around his neck.

"I didn't know. When did it happen?"

"Almost six months ago," he says. "Actually, it was six months ago yesterday. I think I went a little crazy knowing that. He was coming home in two weeks. And they had a mission. It was going to be the last one his unit had to go out on during their deployment. He just had to get through one more."

He stops talking and sucks in a deep breath, his arms wrapped around his knees when he continues.

"But he didn't. Their Humvee hit an IED and that was it. Only two of the guys came home at all."

"What was his name?"

"James."

"I'm so sorry, Doan."

"It's just not right," he says looking up at me, and my heart's breaking again but for completely different reasons now. "It's not fair. James was such a good dude. Better than I'll ever be. Should've been me, you know? But I was too scared to enlist. Didn't want to give up the girls, the drinking, the parties. The freedom. Isn't that funny? I didn't want to give up the one thing my brother was willing to die for. James's dead all so I can go pick up chicks on a Friday at the bar."

"Doan, I -- "

He shakes his head. "Don't, Holly. There's nothing you can say, and nothing you want to say, anyway. Don't feel like you have to."

"I don't feel that way," I tell him. "Not at all. But you know that not everyone is cut out to do the same thing. I know there are a million things Justin is willing to do that I'm not. When we were kids, he saved my life. I almost drowned in our pool and neither of us knew how to swim and he jumped in after me anyway and almost died. I know it isn't the same, but I don't know if I could have done what he did. And I wondered about that everyday for a really long time. I was the one who was drowning. I was the one who was supposed to die, not him. But he almost lost his life, anyway. Protecting me. Kind of like James, I guess."

Doan's staring at me with the strangest of looks on his face.

"What'd you do after that?" he asks.

I shrug. "I was only ten so I don't really remember. But my parents say that I got really quiet for weeks and could barely look at Justin. And when I did talk, I was angry. Always yelling. Always looking for a reason to be mad."

He stays quiet for a second. "I didn't start smoking until James died, you know. I mean, sure, we had some beers and cigarettes before he left, but it didn't really become a thing for me until then. Now I can't stop. I want to, but I can't."

"And the car racing," I say, as I think about how I reacted to Justin saving me. "You do that because of the risk. Because it makes you feel like if something happens to you, you'll get what you think you deserve and that'll somehow make it all better."

Doan looks down at his hands. "It sounds really stupid when you say it like that."

I shrug. "Yeah. Kind of. Because acting like a moron and putting other people at risk isn't smart," I say, and he glances up at me with a small hint of the familiar smile I'm so used to seeing. "But that doesn't mean it doesn't make sense, either."

He furrows his brow. "It doesn't, though."

"Yeah, it does. You said it yourself. You think you should've died instead of your brother. So with the car racing and the smoking and the drinking and all that, you're just being more reckless because you think it should've been you. That isn't gonna help you, though, you know that, right?"

"You sound like my mom," he tells me.

"Smart lady," I say with a smile.

"Yeah."

"Doan, it isn't going to be good for anyone if you get hurt," I tell him. "You've gotta stop doing that stuff."

"Why do you get me like this?" he blurts out. "No one does but you."

I shrug. "Don't know, really. But I could say the same thing about you. You were the one who forced me back into a relationship with my dad, and that's been one of the best things to happen since I moved back here."

"I'm sorry I left you last night," he says then. "It was dumb. I shouldn't have. It's just that I haven't let anyone in since James died, not the way I did with you. I always promised myself I wouldn't do that."

"Well," I say. "If there's one thing I've learned it's that you're pretty good at breaking your promises."

He looks up at me sharply and I offer him a small smile.

"It was just a joke," I say quietly.

"It isn't funny. I don't want to be like that."

"Then change."

"It isn't that easy."

"Why not?"

He doesn't say anything for a few seconds. "Are we over?" he asks me.

"Doan, I don't even know what we are," I say.

"I don't want us to be done," he tells me with such certainty that I have no choice but to believe him.

"You hurt me last night," I say. "That sucked. I was so excited to get up on that stage and know you were there and finally do this thing I've always wanted to do. And you let me down."

"I know," he says. "And I'm -- "

"You told me," I cut in. "You're sorry. And you explained yourself. With a better excuse than I thought you'd have, by the way. But dammit, how do I know this won't happen again?"

"You don't. There are no guarantees," he says. "And maybe there aren't any promises, either. But we have faith and we can have trust."

"Trust in what?"

"What we have. I've never opened myself up to someone the way I have with you. I know I should've told you about James, but I don't talk about him. I've never talked about him more than I have right now," he says. "People out here just knew what happened because they were around when he died. It was never from me."

I think about what he's saying, and I know it's true. I know that from the moment I blurted out to him at the pizza parlor that I might not go to college and the way he understood when I told him about my family that there was something special about Doan Riley and me.

And I'm pretty sure that hasn't gone anywhere.

"I can't promise you that we'll always have this, and I won't. But right now, there's nothing I want more than to be with you. And I can't see that changing."

I fold my hands in front of my lips and stare at him.

With one quick movement, I'm in his arms, and he's wrapping himself around me, his hands stroking my hair and I press my lips against his, and he kisses me back, and I know everything he said is true.

I try to disguise the pounding of my heart against my chest, but it's no use. I can't resist this, can't resist him.

And I haven't been able to since the day I met him.

CHAPTER TWENTY

Six weeks later, I'm finally sitting on the bar stool at Gemma's, the red and blue spotlights shining down on me.

The cast is off my wrist, and it's healed enough so that it doesn't hurt to hold my guitar.

It rests on my lap, song notebook open on the music stand in front of me. I'm wearing the ASU shirt Dad bought me after I told him I'd be enrolling at the school in the fall.

Natalie and Justin and Shane and Dad and Tanya
are all in the audience.

So is Doan.

Everyone I want to see me play for the first time,
with the exception of my mom and the count, is here.

And I can't imagine anything more perfect.

The lights dim, and that's my cue to start.

I strum the first chord, then the second and the third,
and before I know it, I'm hardly thinking about what I'm
doing at all as I start to sing:

"I thought you left me to fall

But maybe I know nothing at

all

Baby you've got me where

you want me

And I'm not going anywhere

I won't make you a promise

Nothing is guaranteed

But if you can trust in us

Maybe you'll see

There's no way to know

If you don't put it out there

Show me you're the one who

cares

And let me steal us a new

home."

The rest of the words tumble out of me like I'm on autopilot and I don't even realize I've finished singing my latest song until cheers and claps and whistles startle me from my daze.

When I look up, Doan's on his feet and I'm pretty sure he's blushing.

Which he should be, since he's obviously the inspiration here.

And as I belt out the next few songs, then get off the stage and run over to him, it's obvious to me now that sometimes the best things happen when we don't think they can.

This move to Arizona felt like the worst thing in the world to me at first.

But I've found a father, a stepmother and a brother, a new friend, and maybe even someone I can see myself with for longer than just a little while.

Everything is new to me here, but it all feels familiar anyway, because I know it's right.

I belong in a place I never thought I could, with a guy I never thought I'd find, and I got back the family I'd left once before.

I'm finally exactly where I want to be.

And I have to say, it feels pretty good.

<<<◇>>>